THE
JIMMY CORKHILL
STORY

THE JIMMY CORKHILL STORY

Adapted from
Phil Redmond's Brookside
by
Rachel Braverman

B🌿XTREE

The publishers would like to thank Sue Mooney
for her help and advice in producing this book.

First published in Great Britain in 1995 by
Boxtree Limited
Broadwall House, 21 Broadwall, London SE1 9PL

ISBN 0 7522 0846 2

10 9 8 7 6 5 4 3 2 1

A CIP catalogue entry for this book is available
from the British Library

Typeset by SX Composing Ltd, Rayleigh, Essex
Printed in Great Britain by Cox & Wyman Limited, Reading, Berks.

Prologue

Jimmy Corkhill was processed quickly out of Walton Jail. The prison officer barely glanced at him as he handed over a few crumpled tenners. Months of scraping pans and scrubbing floors in the kitchens had yielded less than the social would have given him in a week.

Pathetic.

You robbed them on the outside, they robbed you on the inside. Jimmy's lips curled upwards at the thought. Funny that.

"Wipe that grin off your face, Corkhill." Bloody dressed up git couldn't even remember his name without checking his clipboard. "Don't let us see you back in here again."

"No chance." The words came out louder than Jimmy expected. But he meant them. More than he'd ever meant anything in his life.

The screw raised his head, looked Jimmy in the eye. They stared at each other for a moment and the screw lost, dropping his gaze back to his desk and fiddling with the papers.

It was a sign, a tiny triumph. Jimmy had kept his head down, his eyes closed and his mouth shut for five months. He'd achieved the impossible, slipped clean through the system and emerged clear headed and fit the other side. Now, he was on his way. The notes in his pockets were nothing compared to the ones he was going to get. Who said you couldn't beat the system?

The steady walk to the main gate almost drove him mad. Two paces, three, four, stop at the gate, see the key turn, hear the same remarks from the same uniforms in the same deadly, boring, monotonous tone. How could they work there, day in, day out? Didn't they want any excitement, didn't they want to get somewhere in life?

Jimmy could feel his heartbeat get quicker, even though he had to move so slowly. Jackie. In an hour – maybe less – he'd hear her again. The lived in, almost grating voice gave him a thrill, even when she was hurling abuse at him. And she'd had cause to do a lot of that over the years.

Chapter 1

Take the time she'd caught him in his car with Kathy but without his trousers.

"Hiya, love," Jimmy had said, winding the window down. "What're you doing here?"

"What am I doing here? What are you doing without any trousers on? Get dressed. I want you home in five minutes."

He'd never seen her so angry, and that was saying something. Jackie was waiting for him when he slunk round the door.

"Well? What brilliant excuse have you come up with this time?"

"Look, Jack. I can explain. Me pocket got ripped and Kathy was just mending it. Honest, love."

"I've heard some stories in my time, but you beat them all, Jimmy Corkhill."

"It's the truth. You've gotta believe me."

"I do not. God knows why I've put up with you for so long. I want me head examined. But that's it. I'm fed up with it. If you're not down the betting shop or the boozer, you're with some tart. Well, you can get out. Go on. Now. I never want to see you again."

Jimmy found himself bundled into the street. The front door slammed shut behind him.

"Jackie. Have a heart," he pleaded through the letter box. The door opened again. Jimmy was virtually knocked off his feet by a shower of clothes.

"I mean it," Jackie shouted. "And you can take this and all."

His TV landed in a rose bush.

"Watch it. It's fragile, is that." But he was talking to brick walls and lumps of wood.

Oh well, he thought. She'll get over it. She always does. It was her own fault. What'd she been doing in that neck of the woods anyway? In the meantime, there was Kathy. And there'd be no problem with him kipping at their Billy's, because Doreen had just left him.

Having spent the night cowering in the bushes, Jimmy took a random selection of his gear round to Billy's as early as was decent. If he thought he'd find a nice, quiet little gaff, he was in for a shock. Billy was willing enough to let him stay, especially as Jimmy was careful to emphasise the short term, temporary nature of his need for accommodation. Privately, he had a feeling it was going to take longer than usual to get back with Jackie.

He unloaded his cases into the hall and went back for the rest of his stuff. There was always the hope of a quick reconciliation, if he looked really rough. Jackie had a soft heart. She wouldn't see her Jimmy sleeping in the streets.

As it happened, she didn't see him at all. Jimmy banged on the door, but there was no reply. He tried his key. The chain was on, so she was in. She was just playing silly buggers. Right, he thought. Two can play at that game. He'd doss down at Billy's for a couple of nights. Not say a word to her and see how she liked it.

His stuff was stacked neatly outside the front gate right by the bin. It was their day for getting the rubbish collected. If he hadn't got there so early, the binnies would've had the lot.

When Kathy heard what had happened, she went and told her husband about Jimmy. He threw her out. What did she expect? All this honesty only got you into trouble.

Room for one more round at Billy's?

At first, Jimmy was delighted. Kathy was a great girl. Just his type. Trouble was, he still missed Jackie. When her father became dangerously ill he couldn't resist going to see her. Besides, it occurred to him there might be some money in it. The tight old git was rolling in it. Not that anything had come their way. Jimmy hadn't exactly been the perfect son-in-law.

He decided to go for a reconciliation with Jackie, much to Kathy's disgust. Never mind. He'd sort it out with her later.

When he got back to his old council house, he found Jackie crying over her father's photograph.

"Oh it's you," she said. "I might have known you'd show up."

"Ey, Jack, don't be like that." Jimmy felt uncomfortable in his own living room. "I just thought you might fancy a bit of company, like. A shoulder to cry on?"

"What's all this in aid of? You never liked him."

"OK, maybe we never saw eye to eye, but he's your father, isn't he? And you're still me wife, aren't you?"

Jackie burst into floods of tears. Jimmy put his arm round her and wondered why he'd ever left. He forgot it had been Jackie who'd told him to go. So, it seemed, had she. When she suggested that he might perhaps like to come back, just for a while, to help her out, he leapt at the chance.

Surprisingly, the next few days were completely happy for

Jimmy. In her grief, Jackie turned to him for support. The children were miserable anyway, so their hostility to their father somehow faded into the background.

When Jackie's father passed away, she was there to say goodbye and Jimmy was there to hold her hand. All that evening and night she reminisced about him. Jimmy hadn't felt so close to her for years. He loved feeling the weight of her head on his shoulder, her hand on his chest.

Jackie was lying silently in his arms. Talked out, probably. Jimmy couldn't resist broaching the subject of money.

"So what's going to happen to the house, like? And your Mam? Will she move in with your Val or what?"

"God, no." Jackie managed the glimmer of a smile. "Me Mum'll stay where she is. We'll just have to look out for her a bit more, won't we?"

"Yeah. Right. Of course. But what'll she live on? Your Dad put a bit away, didn't he?"

"Yeah. Why?"

"Well, I was wondering, like, what's going to happen to it. I mean, you and Val will get a share, won't you? It's your birthright."

"Me birthright?" Jackie's voice took on that familiar shrill tone. She sat bolt upright. "What on earth are you going on about? Oh, I get it. It's the money, isn't it? You thought you were in with a chance, so you came rushing round here. God, you're incredible, d'you know that? I'm sitting here, trying to get over me father's death and all you're interested in is how much you're going to get out of it."

Jimmy spent the night on the sofa.

They struggled on over the next couple of months. Jimmy did his best, but Jackie was always on his back. Wanting him to come home early like a good little boy, taking all the joy out of a harmless bevvy or two. As for the horses, she got irate if Jimmy so much as passed the betting shop. Of course, Kathy being there might have had something to do with it. It seemed to Jimmy that whichever woman he was with, the other one treated him better.

The rows were depressing, especially for the kids. It got so they seemed to have the same argument, over and over again, about nothing and everything. Mosly they ended up with Jimmy storming off down the pub and Jackie telling him not to come back.

Of course, she didn't mean it. He could always make her laugh. The best way to distract a woman from a man's little foibles. Only one night he came home to find the house dark.

"She's gone to bed," he said to himself, trying to get the key in the lock. He crept upstairs, so as not to wake her, but he needn't have bothered. She wasn't there. Nor were the kids. Nor were any of his things.

He couldn't believe it. Frantically, he threw open the cupboard doors. Empty. Even his underwear drawer. His coat was gone from the hall, his special mug from the kitchen. Jimmy dashed into the living room. All his little bits and pieces, collections of mementoes from years ago, had vanished. There was just space where they used to be. In a panic, he whirled round to face the door. The dartboard. Gone. In its place was a note, pinned with one of his best arrows.

'If you want your clothes, you'll have to buy them back from the Oxfam shop.'

"The bitch," Jimmy muttered through clenched teeth. Then the enormity of what she'd done hit him.

"The bloody bitch," he shouted for all the world to hear.

5

Jimmy spent the day wandering around the house, fuelling his rage with ale. When the phone rang he was incoherent with anger and alcohol. Must be Jackie, he thought, trying to tell her what he thought of her. The phone went dead.

Ten minutes later, Billy showed up.

"What the hell's going on?" he asked, looking around. Somehow, the room had got wrecked. Jimmy was too far gone to answer.

Billy took him back to his. Kathy was still there, the bitch. Laughing at him. He tried to make it up with her. She just pushed him away. Going with his brother, no doubt.

"Bitch." He could hardly get his words out. "Come here."

"Will you get off?" Kathy's face was all misty, but he could tell her mouth was screwed up. "You're drunk. You stink of it."

"You what?" Jimmy was outraged. "My marriage broke up because of you. Don't you get all high and mighty with me."

"Rubbish. You went back and she wouldn't have you. You're making up to me because she's given you the elbow. What do you think I am?"

"I know what you are. We all know what you are. You're a bitch."

There was a struggle of some kind. The next thing Jimmy knew, arms from several different people were hauling him off the sofa and up the stairs.

He woke up in Rod's bedroom, with the biggest hangover of his life. When he remembered what he'd done – what he'd said – he groaned aloud. How was he going to get out of this one? The only possible chance was to lose his memory. It was the drink talking. They always fell for that one.

Kathy wasn't impressed. "Knock it off, Jimmy, will you?

You know what you said. You can't pretend it was just the booze. It won't wash with me."

"Honest to God, Kath. I can't remember anything, honest."

"In vino veritas, Jimmy."

"You what?"

"In wine, the truth. You know what you said, because deep down, you thought it."

Billy was no help. He took Kathy's side completely. There was no getting round them. Jimmy was out on his ear. As he sobered up, the truth hit him. He'd lost his wife, he'd lost his mistress and he was in danger of losing the last of his family. He'd nowhere to go and nothing to do. In despair, he headed for The Swan.

Chapter 2

Jimmy was drowning his sorrows in The Swan. The pub was the one constant in Jimmy's life, a haven he returned to when times were rough. There, he could be sure of a shoulder to cry on and a decent pint. He and The Swan went back a long way. Let's drink to that.

He was determined to get through a load of ale. There was a lot of sorrow to drown. Yet again, he'd lost his home. A scam gone wrong, an irate landlord and Jimmy 'Never Say Die' Corkhill was out on his ear. Another pint would warm him up. Give him the strength to brave the streets.

Sinbad was by his side, supportive and sozzled. Jimmy's companion in failure. They were two of a kind, him and Sinbad – downtrodden members of the underprivileged working class. No wonder they never got anywhere. There was always some snotty git with a posh accent and a suit, waiting to smash them in the face. It wasn't the first time he and Sinbad had faced the streets, and it probably wouldn't be the last. Sinbad had it worse, though, brought up in the local orphanage. He'd never known the closeness of family. At least Jimmy had that. Poor old Sinbad. Get another drink in. Forget your troubles.

But now Jimmy seemed to be losing his relations. Billy had taken up with Sheila Grant – a pious, narrow minded woman who was always going on about what was right and proper. Hardly the kind to welcome Jimmy as a brother-in-law. She'd got a nerve, though. Called herself a Catholic, but that hadn't stopped her getting divorced. She hadn't much to boast about with her son, either. Barry Grant was the local hard man, a successful villain and a bully. He was making Billy's life a misery. Didn't want his precious mother mixed up with the Corkhills. Who was he to judge them?

If you wanted respectability what could be better than Tracy and Rod, Billy's kids? A hairdresser and a policeman. Who was Barry Grant to look down on a family complete with its own woodentop? The cheek of it. And for all his threats and fine words, Barry wasn't a patch on Frankie. There'd never been anyone like Frankie. Jimmy could feel the tears welling up. Whenever he was well and truly pissed, he remembered his big brother. Sober, it was like he had a metal door in his mind. Don't look behind here. Don't think about him. Don't get angry. It doesn't do any good. Alcohol melted the barrier. The only way out was more beer and stupor.

Through the haze in his mind Jimmy thought he could see a familiar figure at the bar. The round, bald head, the prominent eyes, the strained sinews at the neck, the way his face seemed to be all grey. It couldn't be. Joey Godden? Here?

"It's all this beer," he slurred to Sinbad. "Giving me hallucinations."

He stared. Then he heard the laugh. The one that had always infuriated him. The one that had killed Frankie in the end. It was pure mockery. A laugh that said, 'I'm here and there's nothing you can do about it.' Ha. Ha. Ha. There was no joke. Except the one on the Corkhills.

Jimmy found himself on his feet and at the bar. When he

got close up, he realised it wasn't the ale. This was for real. Godden was out. Fifteen years in the slammer had sucked in his cheeks, pulled the skin tight across his skull, pushed his eyes out even more. But inside nothing had changed – for anyone.

"What are you doing here?" Jimmy spluttered.

Godden took a slow sup from his glass. He looked Jimmy straight in the eye.

"Boo," he said. The no-mark didn't even have the grace to be frightened. Just stood there, like he owned the place.

Jimmy leapt on him. He had no choice. All he could think was that this murderer was alive and free, while Frankie was dead. He lunged forward, determined to get his hands round Godden's throat. Sinbad, fat and worried, tugged at his arm. "Jimmy, are you trying to get us killed or what?"

"There's only one person going to get killed around here. And that's him."

But the beer had made him too unsteady to be effective. He let Sinbad drag him out, Godden's insults ringing in his ear. Let him laugh. He'd be laughing on the other side of his face soon enough.

As soon as he was sober, Jimmy was round at Billy's. They had to do something. Take revenge. Instead, all Billy wanted to do was wallow in nostalgia. Reminisce about Frankie handing out the ciggies. And Mam holding his hand while he bled to death.

"We've got to do something," said Jimmy. "We owe Joey Godden for both Frankie and me mam."

There was a pause. Both of them were fifteen years away, at a winter graveside.

"I'll never forget the day he was buried," Jimmy broke the silence. "I made him a promise, Bill. On his grave."

"I know," said Billy.

"So how're we going to do it then?"

"What?"

Jimmy started to feel uneasy. It was obvious what they had to do. "Get Joey Godden."

"It's a long time ago, Jim."

"Fifteen years. Frankie could have had a wife or a family by now."

"He wasn't the settling down type."

"He didn't get the chance to, did he?"

"We'll have to think about it."

Think about it. What was there to think about? Jimmy was outraged, betrayed. Their brother's murderer was on the loose and all Billy could do was think about it. What about the promise? They'd both promised to avenge Frankie. They couldn't go back on their word now.

"They were funeral promises." Billy sounded tired. "We were both a lot younger then."

Jimmy couldn't believe what he was hearing. Billy was trying to get out of it. "This is family, Billy. Blood's thicker than water, you know."

"But it's not going to bring Frankie back. We've got families of our own to think about now."

They argued for hours. Jimmy had never felt so let down. It was like a real, physical sinking feeling in his stomach. He'd always assumed he and Billy thought the same. Now it seemed they were miles apart. His brother, his own flesh and blood, was a coward and a liar. Frankie, Mam, Jimmy himself. None of them mattered to Billy any more.

Jimmy couldn't get Godden out of his mind. Drinking was no good. Godden had installed himself in The Swan. When

Jimmy tried The British Lion, the grinning skull was there again. He would have crippled him there and then, only Godden had the sense not to go in alone. It was just like the old days: Godden and gang against the Corkhills. Except now Jimmy was on his own. Frankie was dead and Billy was hiding behind common sense and apron strings.

"It's all in the past," he said. "I'm just interested in the present."

As far as Jimmy was concerned, he was talking crap. Of course this was the present. That bastard was sitting in their local the same as he was fifteen years ago. Nothing had changed. Nothing had been sorted.

If Billy wouldn't help him, he'd have to do it alone. Wait for that no – mark to take one step by himself, then bang, that'd be it. Then Jimmy could get on with his life.

He tooled up in Billy's spare room. All the gear. He had a knot in the pit of his stomach. It was the thought of going in there by himself. And somewhere at the back of his mind was the knowledge that he was fifteen years older and slower. His hands were shaking. Threading the shoelaces was impossible. He was all thumbs and elbows.

"Get in there," he muttered.

Kathy would choose that moment to make an entrance. She could have helped, but no. All she would do was stand around and ask damn fool questions.

"What are you doing?"

What did it look like? "Going fishing," he replied. He asked her to lace his shoes. A small job. Something he'd have thought a woman could cope with. They were taught to thread needles in school, weren't they? Kathy just stood there with the shoes in her hand, winding up for a good old nag.

She knew what he was about to do. What she didn't realise was why. She didn't understand. None of them did.

Jimmy tried to explain. "Our kid would be walking the streets, alive, today, if it wasn't for that scumbag, right?"

"Your Frankie would be standing here telling you to take all that stupid gear off, if he was walking around alive today."

What did she know? She'd never met him. Only heard the rumours. Frankie would have been in there the moment he'd seen Godden's ugly mug. He wouldn't have given a load of bull about the past and water under bridges. If it had been Billy or Jimmy that had got it all those years ago, Frankie would have kept his anger going and taken his revenge. It was up to Jimmy to deal with Godden now.

"I'll tell you what I'm doing," Jimmy said. "I am going to break his fingers. Because he's had two of them up to the Corkhills ever since he got out. And then when he's counting his fingers, I'm going to break his head. Alright?"

"Jimmy, no." Kathy came out with everything she could. Frankie was dead, so it didn't matter. Jimmy'd never get away with it. Having Godden look over his shoulder for the rest of his life would be a better revenge. All rubbish. Total crap. "Think about it, will you?" she begged. "Just think about what you're doing."

"I'm doing it because Frankie was me big brother," said Jimmy. "I swore to him, lying in his coffin. He didn't look small or faded away or anything. Not like he died when he was an old man. He was still as big as he'd ever been. He was me big brother."

If she didn't understand now, she never would.

Godden wasn't hard to find. The difficulty was getting him

on his own. He knew Jimmy would be after him. He'd be expecting Billy as well. For three days, he never took a step without his two henchmen.

It wasn't till closing time on Friday night that Jimmy got lucky. Out rolled Godden and his lads, weaving around and laughing like maniacs. Godden had his arm round a tart. They started to kiss, leaning up against the wall of the public bar. It was a long, long smooch and Godden's other companions were getting restless.

"Go on, boys." Godden came up for air. "Home. I'll be alright. I've got company."

"OK."

"You're the boss."

They wandered away. By now, the pub was empty. The only people in the car park were Godden, the bird – and Jimmy. Stone cold sober and furious. How could he fail? He took a baseball bat from his bag.

"Hey, Godden," he shouted. "I wanna word with you."

"Jimmy Corkhill." Godden pushed the girl to one side. "What a pleasant surprise. Fancy seeing you here."

"You won't in a minute. I'm going to do you. Like you did our Frankie."

He was about to charge when his arms were grabbed from behind. The bat went flying.

"Guess who?" It was Godden's guards.

Godden himself was standing dead still, no trace of the booze about him. The girl had vanished.

"Did you think I'd wait for you to put the boot in?" Godden strolled over to where the bat had landed. He picked it up. "I'm getting tired of seeing your shadow every time I look round."

Jimmy saw the bat swing up above Godden's shoulder. He fought to free himself and managed to get in a couple of good kicks before the bat came down with a loud crack. There was a sharp, explosive pain in his chest. He dropped to the ground, too winded to get up. The next few minutes were a painful blur. The only sounds were his own groans and the grunts of his attackers. A boot landed across his forehead and he tasted blood. All he could do was cower, curled up, hands across his face-roll over to try and escape the blows. No use. They kept coming and coming. Soon, his whole body was screaming in agony. His leg was at an angle and he could hardly breathe.

As he blacked out, he heard Godden's voice in his ear.

"The feud's not over yet, Corkhill."

Chapter 3

Jimmy woke up in hospital, sore and bitter. Four cracked ribs and a broken leg meant he felt like he was being knifed every time he laughed or coughed or breathed. Worse, though, was the ache left by Billy's betrayal. He wasn't there when he needed him the most.

At visiting time, Jimmy poured his heart out to his one remaining brother. Billy was unrepentant, still full of "what's the point?", "times move on" and "people change".

"Frankie wasn't like us, you know," he said. "He'd fight and make sure we were never short of a few bob, but he needed to do it his way. You know that. Sometimes he was a bully and decent people – people who hadn't done anything – were frightened of him . . . He loved it. I've always tried to sort things out by working for a living. Yeah, we could jump on Godden one night, knock seven bells out of him, kill him even, but it's not my way. Violence only leads to violence. That's why you're here. Just let go, will you?"

Stuck in a hospital bed, Jimmy had no choice. For the moment. Billy might have chosen a different path, but *he* would always remain loyal to Frankie. The problem was, he didn't seem to be up to it. Besides, Godden's last words to him rang in his ears and woke him up sweating every night. Jimmy knew it was by no means over.

At least he had somewhere comfortable to convalesce. Billy installed him in the extension. It was great at first, being waited on hand and foot. Sheila seemed to have melted a bit. Kathy was nicer to him than she had been in ages. Even tucked him in. Sinbad visited, Rod and Tracy popped in to chat.

Billy and Sheila were planning to get married. A summer wedding – 10th August. Jimmy decided to take charge. He could make phone calls from his sick bed and go to town when he was up and hobbling about. The happy couple said they wanted a quiet do, but everyone always says that. When they see the marquee and the food and the cake and the drink flowing, they're delighted.

Everyone was a bit short of the old readies, so Jimmy had to call in a few favours. A bloke he'd supplied with some very cheap rope returned the favour by diverting a marquee in Jimmy's direction. He got the cake at a knock down price. The sandwiches would be supplied by a caterer, who had reason to be grateful for some business Jimmy had put his way. Smoked salmon, too. Couldn't get much posher than that.

Jimmy was glad to do it. He and Billy were closer than they had been for weeks. When Billy got an attack of the jitters, they had a real heart to heart.

"You and Frankie were all I ever had to look up to," Jimmy told him. "Now, it's only you and me."

Billy warned him not to put people on pedestals, but hero worship was as natural to Jimmy as breathing. And sometimes as painful as breathing through broken ribs. He saw Billy, the family man, with his kids and his new fiancée, and couldn't help feeling left out. What had he done with his life? What had Jimmy Corkhill achieved? A big nothing . . . he was a failure. Both Frankie and Billy saw what they wanted and went after it. Somehow Jimmy, the lad, the good laugh, always got distracted.

But Godden was never out of Jimmy's mind. He was convinced that he'd pull some stunt over their Billy's wedding. Jimmy took the precaution of hiring Sinbad to provide a bit of muscle. Well, flab. But from a distance he looked mean enough. Jimmy gave him a few pointers from his own experience and The *Godfather* films. Also, he'd arranged for seven men to be dressed in suits. Any sign of trouble and he'd be able to pick on a few able bodies to help out.

The big day dawned and 10 Brookside Close became a madhouse. People were coming and going with presents and good wishes. It was great. Even Jimmy had forgotten to be suspicious when he heard a knock at the door one morning. Stuck to the knocker was an enormous wreath: yellow and white carnations in a ring. A purple banner across it read 'Billy And Sheila. RIP'. Jimmy's first reaction was pure fury. What kind of psychopath sends a wreath to a wedding? But he couldn't go haring off after Godden. He shoved the thing into the extension. Godden would have to wait.

Jimmy was proud of his arrangements. There were one or two little hitches, a few minor details, like there being no wine for the more refined. A quick call to Billy Carter sorted that out. OK, so the suits didn't exactly fit the men, but once they'd been swapped round a bit, they looked a million dollars. No one was going to get that close to them, anyway. The sandwiches were a bit more tricky. The trouble with fish is that you can't risk eating it after the sell-by date. Certainly not more than a week after. Ever resourceful, Jimmy organised an assembly line and they had enough food for an army in no time. As for the cake, a few blows from a chisel and you'd never know it had been meant for Dave and Liz.

The most difficult problem was the cars. Jimmy could have kicked himself for forgetting them. He even knew someone who could get hold of a stretch limo. Couldn't be helped. They ended up piling into a neighbour's car. Frank Rogers was a good man, but a nut about his old Cortina. Of course, it had to break down, right in the middle of the high street. Billy ended up legging it half a mile to the registry office, only just in time to stop Sheila storming off.

Jimmy arrived as the registrar told the bride and groom to have a snog. You don't get much for your money with these civil services, do you? Still, they looked dead happy. Sheila threw her bouquet into the crowd and Jimmy ended up catching it. Everyone thought this was a great laugh, but it made him think.

As the cars took them back to the house, Jimmy was quiet. He'd recovered from his injuries and didn't have an excuse to stay at Billy's now. The newly-weds would hardly want him there. Where could he go? Jackie had the council house, renting was too expensive and his credit didn't run to mortgages. Kathy was sitting beside him, happy and radiant. She had a good, steady job and she loved him. Most of the time. There wasn't room for both of them at her sister's, but perhaps it was time he made an honest woman of her.

The garden looked a treat, with table cloths and flags and banners. Jimmy went down on bended knee to Kathy and proposed. He was honest about his reasons. Start as you mean to go on. Just proved his theory. She told him to sod off, but nicely. He got up, brushed his knees and went back to the party.

Cousin Don showed up. Jimmy was delighted, except he'd actually come to pick up the suits. A slight detail about them having to get back to the cleaners, their owner was coming to pick them up. Don was a pushover. A few bevvies and he'd have stayed all week. Out of the corner of his eye, Jimmy spotted Kathy laughing her head off at his negotiating technique. He knew he was on to a winner so he tried again, this time suggesting they find a flat together. To his amazement, she said yes. Make 'em laugh. Works every time.

The only sour note to the entire day was Barry Grant. He wasn't happy about his mother's marriage and told Billy so in no uncertain terms. It seemed he hadn't changed his mind about the Corkhills. Jimmy was worried that Godden would show up, and prove Barry right. Luckily, the wreath proved to be Godden's only bad will gesture.

Unfortunately, Billy found it a week later. He waited till he and Jimmy were alone before having it out with him. They were in the kitchen, doing the washing up of all things. Jimmy was trying to make a good impression.

"Maybe I should bring Rod in on this," Billy said.

"Why? What's it got to do with him?"

"He's a bizzie, isn't he?"

"Well, go on then. Tell him, if you think it'll do any good. Go ahead." Jimmy was exasperated with his brother's shortsightedness. "You'll put the lad in a no-win situation. His superiors know Godden. They'll probably blow on more. No one else is going to sort this out, but us. It's got nothing to do with Rod, anyway, so why involve him?"

"I want a clean slate with this marriage." Billy concentrated hard on drying a wooden spoon.

"So you keep saying. There's only one way you're going to get it."

Billy's next suggestion was that he should talk to Godden. Clear the air. You forget about us and we'll forget about you. Jimmy couldn't believe his ears. What was he going to do? Apologise for Frankie's stomach getting in the way of his knife fifteen years ago?

Again, Jimmy had the uneasy feeling that he was the big brother. "Billy. Grow up, will you?" he said. "There's a nutter out there. A fella who murdered our brother. He's not used to listening or understanding or reason. No one in their right mind would send a wreath to the bride and groom on their wedding day."

"It was a warning, that's all."

"Too right it was. You can't reason with a killer, Billy!" Jimmy used the washing-up brush for emphasis. "He only understands one thing – retaliation. And if we don't get our retaliation in first, we've had it. When are you going to learn mate – it's us or him."

"Who do you think you are? Wyatt Earp?" Billy's voice was high with tension. "I don't want Sheila involved in feuds, fights and god knows what. I'm a married man. I just want to get on with my life, right?"

"Me too, only Godden doesn't see it that way, does he?" said Jimmy. "I've told you, Billy. He's off his head. He's nuts. He murdered our Frankie and I'll tell you something else. He is not going to rest until he's killed off the rest of the family. Think about it."

Billy told Rod and, of all people, Barry Grant. Rod got one of his bosses to have a quiet word with Godden, but things only got worse. Jimmy and Billy were banned from The Swan and The British Lion. Godden was causing grief, but the police promised they'd pull the Corkhills in as well at the first sign of trouble. Jimmy was livid.

Even Barry joined in the chorus of "let it go", "it's over" and "forget it". He didn't think Jimmy had enough balls to face up to Godden. He'd have to think again.

No way on earth was Jimmy going to let that bastard take over his locals. The next day, he took Kathy to The Swan. Don was there too. Jimmy drank steadily, purposefully, watching Godden's performance to the bar maid.

Kathy looked worried. "I've never seen you drink like this. What's up?"

She looked across, saw Godden and worked out who he was. His barking laugh was aimed straight at their table.

Ha. Ha. Ha.

Jimmy couldn't stand it any longer.

"He's laughing at me."

He felt Kathy reach for his arm, heard her terrified "Jimmy, don't", but this time he'd had enough. More than enough. This time Godden was history.

Don got up with him. He'd be loyal to Frankie. Best mates last. All the scams they'd been through together. It counted.

Jimmy and Don leapt on Godden. His mates leapt on them. There was a fight, a blur of fists and kicks. Jimmy was exhilarated, his blood singing. He got a crack or two at Godden and was about to put the boot in when everything suddenly went quiet. The hands let go and each man was standing by himself. Billy appeared at Jimmy's elbow, summoned by Kathy. He was looking at a body on the floor. Don was lying in a pool of blood, his head split open on the bar rail. They didn't need the ambulance and the bizzies to tell them he was dead.

Chapter 4

It was Don's death finally convinced Billy something had to be done about Godden. However, he insisted on planning everything carefully. He always was the forward planner. Jimmy was the feet first merchant. If anything happened to Godden, the Corkhills would be first in the frame, so they had to arrange alibis.

Jimmy had a word with the owner of the local sauna. Alfie Barker would be only too happy to help a regular customer, especially one who knew as much as Jimmy did about some of the services offered. It was perfect.

They arrived outside Godden's house with their gear. Revenge was so close Jimmy found himself shaking. His palms leaked sweat till he could hardly grip the baseball bat. He swallowed a couple of times, trying to get some moisture into his mouth.

Billy looked just as bad. "Scared?" he said.

Jimmy nodded. He and Billy clasped each other's hands. Brothers again at last. They agreed they were doing the right thing. There was no other way to get it sorted.

"For our Frankie," said Jimmy.

"For our Frankie," Billy agreed.

They crept towards the house, ready for action. A car pulled up outside, causing them to merge into a hedge. Three men got out and rang the bell. It couldn't be true. Godden was getting reinforcements. Jimmy craned his neck to get a look at them.

"Alfie Barker. The bastard."

Billy was furious. "You even told him what time we'd be here," he hissed.

"I told him the time, so he could say we were with him. He knows we're after Joey Godden. He must have put two and two together."

They slunk off, the sound of laughter drifting down the garden path after them. Ha. Ha. Ha.

Godden wasn't finished with them yet. It got worse. First, he sent a mass card to Sheila, another example of his sick sense of humour. But worse was to come.

In the middle of a Saturday afternoon a white pickup stopped outside Billy's house. Without warning the living room window was smashed to pieces as a huge heavy slab was heaved through it. There on the carpet, surrounded by glass fragments, was Frankie's tombstone.

IN LOVING MEMORY
FRANCIS CORKHILL
BORN OCTOBER 11TH 1942
DIED JULY 17TH 1975
AND THEY SHALL REST IN PEACE

Only Godden wasn't letting them rest in peace. Jimmy's blood boiled with frustration and rage. There was nothing he could do. Nothing. That no-mark was running rings round his family, driving them to despair and all he could do was stamp his foot and shout. Useless.

Rod talked to his bosses again and there was a family conference to hear the result. Jimmy couldn't help feeling uneasy when Barry Grant was included. He unnerved him.

The bizzies were no help. Jimmy never thought they would be.

"I've been on to the CID," said Rod. "They reckon you were as much to blame as Godden."

It was outrageous. "You what?" said Jimmy. "It's not us who go around desecrating graves. Throwing tombstones through people's windows."

"I'm only telling you what he said," Rod replied. "If you make a formal complaint, Godden will be questioned."

"Questioned? He should be locked up, him." Jimmy couldn't stay in his seat. His fury kept him pacing the room.

"Let the lad finish." Billy was trying to calm things down, as usual.

Rod continued. "He'll be questioned and they'll probably release him. As it's your word against his and due to the history of violence between you, it's highly doubtful they'd believe you. It's your word against his, so they probably wouldn't proceed."

"So the top and bottom of it is, the bizzies'll do nothing." At last, Billy was getting the point.

"If anything happens to us, they take Godden in," said Rod. "If anything happens to him, they take you two in. I could end up arresting me own father and uncle. This has got to stop here and now, Dad."

Sheila came up with a bright suggestion. She would go and talk to Godden. Tracy said she'd go with her. It drove Jimmy mad that they couldn't see how futile that was. You can't reason with a nutter. You've got to play him at his own game. Billy said he wanted Sheila to go to her sister's in Basingstoke.

"I'm not going anywhere without you." Sheila's quiet voice was more convincing than any scream.

Barry made his first contribution to the discussion. "Look what a mess you've got her into, Billy." He was only bothered about his mother getting involved.

"Stop it, Barry." Sheila was firm with her son. "Alright, if you don't want me to talk to Godden, let's just forget all about it. What Rod says makes sense about the police. If Godden knows that, then he's not going to do anything else stupid, is he? Let's start looking forward instead of back."

And that was as far as they got. Action to be taken? None. Jimmy wanted to put his fist through a wall, he was so frustrated. As he stormed out, he noticed Barry had brought in a sports holdall. Nothing odd about that, except that he never went too far away from it, as if there was an invisible chain linking it to his hand.

When the room was empty, Jimmy opened the bag. It contained a shotgun. He showed it to Billy, who had it out with him.

"I'm making sure that no one I care about ends up in a coffin." Barry was soft spoken, like his mother. Only everything he said carried a threat.

Billy was capable of being firm when it counted. "The gun goes," he said.

"You've made a right mess of it so far, haven't you?" retorted Barry.

This was too much for Jimmy. "And what would you do about it, eh?"

"I wouldn't have let it get this far, would I? Look, Godden's no one. I know he pulled a knife, but he couldn't get a job walking greyhounds for the big boys. You didn't know that, did you?"

"The gun stays in the bag in the house," Billy repeated.

"You do it your way, and I'll do it mine." With that, Barry stalked off.

"What are you going to do about it?" Jimmy asked.

"Get Sheila well out of the way, that's for sure," replied Billy.

Jimmy felt his heart skip a beat with fear. Sheila had already said she wouldn't go anywhere without Billy, so what was he going to do? Go with her? Abandon his home, his roots, his family? If he left, Jimmy would have no one. Kathy was great, but she wasn't family. Not in the way Billy was.

His fears proved justified. Within a week, Sheila and Billy had arranged a place in Basingstoke for themselves and for Tracy and Rod to take over the house. Before they left, Billy tried one last time to make Jimmy drop the feud.

"At least think about it," he pleaded.

"You want me to make it easy for you," said Jimmy, bitterly. "Leave your worries behind you and a nice rosy future ahead. That's why you want me to say that I'll think about it, eh?"

"Too right. That's just what I want you to do. It's for your own sake, Jim. I mean, it's tearing Kathy apart and it's tearing Sheila apart. Just let it go and we can go away from here without worrying about anyone."

"What if we get another special delivery?"

"The bizzies'll rip into him. I'm going away from here to show that I'm doing something about it. If he does anything stupid, then he'll have to pay the consequences." Billy sighed. "All I'm asking you to do is not to cause any more trouble, Jim."

Jimmy felt hopeless. Defeated. His brother was deserting him and he couldn't do or say anything to stop him. "Alright,

Billy," he said. "You can sail away from here and live happily ever after as far as I'm concerned. Just hope that if you don't go after him, he doesn't come after you."

Jimmy was choked when it came to saying goodbye. Billy's battered old Cortina was so packed they could hardly see out of the back window.

As the car turned the corner, Barry pulled a bullet out of his pocket and held it to Jimmy's temple. "I'm going to show you how to deal with the likes of Godden," he said.

He was back a few days later.

"You'll have no more problems with him," he announced.

Jimmy wanted to know what he'd done, but Barry wouldn't be drawn.

"With fellas like him, they need someone their own size to take them on, don't they?" was all he'd say.

Jimmy's pride was hurt. He was now head of the family. It was up to him to take Godden out. Barry hadn't even given him a chance. "Listen. I could have sorted that," he protested.

"Like you did last time? When somebody ended up getting killed?" Barry's voice was heavy with sarcasm. He refused to say how he'd done it and Jimmy was left to fume by himself.

The whole episode left Jimmy restless and unhappy. Whatever Barry had done, it had worked. He had pressed the right buttons, made the right contacts. Jimmy didn't even come close. Kathy did her best to help, but her cooing sympathy got on his nerves. She was too obviously pleased and relieved that peace had been restored.

Jimmy couldn't concentrate. What little money he did manage to make went straight into the boozer's till. It soon ran out. Used to a tight budget, Kathy made sure she always had enough to pay the bills. She kept jars in the kitchen cupboard, labelled rent, gas and electricity. They weren't due for ages. She wouldn't mind if Jimmy borrowed a bit. Just for a few days, till he was on his feet again. No point in mentioning it to her. He'd have it back before she noticed.

Only it didn't work out like that. First it was a couple of quid from the gas, then a fiver from the rent. Before he knew where he was, the jars were empty. Jimmy tried to cover up by hiding the brown envelopes when they dropped through the door. He could make it up with one decent horse. Given Kathy's job in his local bookies, he sneaked off to a betting shop miles away to place his last note on a dead cert. It came in last. Jimmy had to go home and face the music.

Kathy didn't say a lot. In fact, she was too busy screaming to form actual words. When she picked up a heavy ashtray Jimmy knew it was time to scarper.

He headed straight for Billy's place. Rod was there, but wouldn't cover for his favourite uncle. Young people these days have no character. Kathy came charging round, banging on the door and playing havoc with the bell. Jimmy locked himself in the bathroom and waited for her to go.

It soon became clear that she was settled in for a siege. In desperation, Jimmy shinned down the drainpipe and hopped over the fence. He found himself nose to nose with a heavily built, middle-aged man, who'd just moved in next door. Ron Dixon proved he was a fine addition to the neighbourhood by offering sanctuary.

Jimmy managed to get back into the house safely enough, but Kathy was waiting for him the next time he put his nose out the back door. She cracked him a good one across the jaw. As far as she was concerned, enough was enough. She wanted

Jimmy out of her life. The most he could get her to agree to was that she'd consider taking him back if he could replace the money he'd nicked.

Promise them anything, then work out how to get out of it, had always been Jimmy's motto. Then, for the first time in ages, he had a stroke of luck. Rod and Tracy both went on holiday, leaving him in sole charge of the house. Neither would be back for a couple of weeks. It was a golden opportunity. As soon as he'd seen them both off, Jimmy got hold of a van and pawned every item that could be shifted.

In spite of herself, Kathy was highly amused at his way out of the situation. And he had kept his promise. There was even enough money left over for fish and chips. They used a dilapidated green armchair as a table. It was the only piece of furniture left.

"Possessions possess," said Jimmy through a mouthful of cod. "Once you get a hold of things you've got responsibilities, haven't you? You've got to look after things." It was his biggest dilemma. On the one hand, he wanted the comfort of objects round him. On the other, they tied you down. Choked you, if you weren't careful.

"You wouldn't know a responsibility if it jumped up and took a bite out of your left leg," Kathy laughed.

"And who was it who's just gone and sorted out all the bills?"

"Yeah. And got the money to pay for it with his own brother's furniture. That's not the actions of a responsible person."

"It shows that I think on my feet, that I'm a survivor."

Kathy sighed. "But you're the one that keeps wrecking the boats."

Jimmy had to admit it was true. The conversation was getting depressing, so they started to reminisce.

"D'you remember flouncing out through the door that time?" Funny how Jimmy always remembered the arguments best. "You got your dressing gown caught in it, didn't you? I was left looking at this piece of cloth, thinking I'm sure she's gonna come back in. And I'm trying to keep me face straight, 'cos all the while I'm thinking, if she comes in and finds me laughing, she'll have me."

"You should have seen your face." Kathy was in a mellower mood now.

"When I opened it. And there was nothing there but an empty dressing gown lying on the floor. The incredible shrinking woman. We've had some good times, haven't we kid?"

"Some terrible rows." She sounded like she was about to cry.

"And now for my next trick . . ." Jimmy tried to cheer her up, but the magic wasn't working. There was a long pause.

"For my next trick, I'm going to disappear." Kathy was deadly serious. "I thought you might start thinking it's about time you began to act your age. You're 38. All these stupid scams, mixing with scum like Godden."

"That's all over. I promise you. It is. Honest." Promise anything. Make your excuses later – if you can.

"I don't think so. I'm banging my head against a brick wall. I've had enough."

"What about all the good times? Who makes you laugh like I do?"

"Nobody. Nobody makes me cry as much as you do, either. I'll tell you what. If it's alright with you, I'll just take the laughs."

"You can't just go." Jimmy started to panic.

Kathy got up and walked slowly to the door. "What's stopping me?" she said. "Now you see me . . ."

She closed the door behind her without even finishing her sentence. And that was the last Jimmy ever saw of her.

Chapter 5

After Kathy left, Jimmy found himself doing the dreary round of rented flats and bedsits. He hit rock bottom when he moved in with Sinbad. The gaff was so small, they had to sleep in bunk beds. Neither was any good at housekeeping and the place was always full of dirty dishes and smelly socks.

It was so depressing Jimmy spent every spare minute round with Rod and Tracy. Or even just in the house, if they weren't there. The only problem with that was that Julia bloody Brogan, Billy's mother-in-law, was staying with the Dixons next door. She was as common as the rest of them, with an accent you could cut with a knife, but she had pretensions. Jimmy had never got on with her, any more than he had with her snotty daughter, Doreen.

Most of the time he could avoid her, but one afternoon she positively sought him out. What did he think of young Lindsey's marriage?

Lindsey? Married? She couldn't. She was just a child.

Jimmy was stunned. He sat down at the kitchen table, his mouth dropped open, unable to say a thing. In the background, he could hear Julia's irritating jabber, but the words merged into one big mockery. His little girl was getting wed and no one had bothered to tell him. Not Lindsey. Not Jackie. Certainly not Jimmy Junior. He'd had to hear it from some nosy old cow.

Why hadn't they told him? He was her father. He had a right to know. He was supposed to escort her down the aisle, wasn't he? The proudest moment of a father's life. It hit him like a cold, sopping sponge. Jackie had another fella now, didn't she. A newsagent, Ken Summers. He'd been her boss, but had lost no time getting his feet under the table. What if Lindsey had asked him to give her away instead of Jimmy?

She wouldn't do that. Not his little Lindsey. Only she wasn't so little now. Jimmy realised with a shock that she was nineteen. Not too young to get married at all. In fact, Jackie had been a year younger than that when they'd wed. Another generation had grown up. Suddenly, Jimmy felt the full force of almost forty years. The big Four Zero was catching up with him. November would see him facing middle age, and what had he got to show for it? Nothing.

Back at Sinbad's, Jimmy brooded for hours. OK, he hadn't been around in the last few years. That wasn't his fault though, was it? Jackie hadn't let him near them. And with a new fella round the place, Jimmy hadn't stood a chance.

In desperation, he decided to write to Lindsey, to beg her forgiveness and make peace. If she knew how much sweat had gone into the letter, she'd be round like a shot. She must be. He had to give her away. It was his right.

The next problem was the usual one. Money. He'd need a fair bit to get kitted out properly. Suit. Tie. Haircut. The works. Lindsey would be proud of him. If he could find the dosh.

DD Dixon, Ron's wife, seemed to be the answer to his prayers. He found her looking worriedly across the lawn. It seemed she'd forgotten her and Ron's anniversary. And Jimmy had always thought it was the men that did that. What DD needed was a garden ornament. Could Jimmy find one?

Is the Pope Catholic? Best not say that to DD, who was another of those terrifyingly devout women. Yes, of course he could oblige. Anything for a neighbour. No problem.

The Dixon's garden was a fair old size, so your average gnome wouldn't do. Jimmy thought about it for a while, and came up with a brainwave. Roscoe Park. It was full of stone bits and pieces. Great big things that everyone ignored. Probably be weeks before anyone noticed one was missing. Jimmy went for a wander and found exactly what he was looking for. There was a stone lion set back from the main paths, close to the swings and, more importantly, the perimeter fence. Half hidden by trees and covered in moss, it was a sorry sight. However, a touch of the old elbow grease and it'd look a million dollars. Especially round at Ron Dixon's.

Jimmy borrowed a pick-up and sneaked into the park after dark. The bloody animal weighed a ton, but eventually it was loaded up. Jimmy spent the night cleaning it and got it to the Dixons'.

"What d'you reckon to that?" he said proudly to DD.

She wasn't amused. Some people have got no class. OK, so it was a bit on the big side and she hadn't expected a full size king of the jungle to turn up on her lawn, but he'd done what she'd asked. No way was he going to take it back. As for a refund, she could forget it.

As if DD wasn't hassle enough, Jimmy started getting a hard time from Sinbad. Seems he recognised the lion. Part of his childhood. When Sinbad got on to his childhood the weeping violins began to play. Trouble was, Jimmy was a sucker for it. He could just picture the kids from the orphanage playing around Lenny the Lion, stroking his nose, making wishes. Having a whale of a time.

Jimmy gave in. He'd put the ruddy animal back. Another round of sweating and strain and doing his back in and it was loaded up. So far, so good. He drove back to the park, swearing under his breath. Right outside the gates was a squad car loaded with bizzies. Jimmy panicked. He dumped the van under some trees and legged it in the opposite direction. A hundred yards later, he felt the old hand on the shoulder.

The cell where he spent the night was freezing. No food. No ale. Nothing but his own thoughts to keep him company. His life flashed before him with horrible clarity. He'd done nothing. He'd seen nothing. Nothing worked for him. Everything he touched fell apart. Now Lindsey, his only daughter, was getting married and she hadn't even been going to tell him.

Jimmy found himself pacing up and down to keep warm, like some caged lion. He was a failure. There was no other word for it. He was nearly forty. He'd lost his family. He couldn't even make it as a robber. It was the most miserable night of his life.

He was released on bail in the morning. There would be a fine, but God knew how he was going to pay it. At least Sinbad proved to be a mate, listening for hours as Jimmy poured his heart out.

"I know I let Jackie down, but I never let the kids down," he said.

"You never saw them, did you?" replied Sinbad.

"She wouldn't let me near the place. She even sent their birthday cards back. In the end, I just stopped trying."

"No. You shouldn't've."

There was a long pause. Jimmy knew he hadn't really tried very hard. He'd only sent cards the first year. Jackie was still furious with him then. She would have calmed down, she always did. The truth was, he simply hadn't bothered. It was down to him to sort it out. Nobody else. And he hadn't thought twice about them.

"And now look what's happening. Lindsey's getting married." Jimmy had reached the height of despair. "What happens when a girl gets married? You have a wedding. The father walks the daughter up the aisle. All proud and that. He makes a speech saying how great she is, how much he loves her. I want to do all that when our Lindsey gets married, but someone else is going to walk her up the aisle. Someone else is going to make that speech, aren't they? I'm not even invited. Let's face it, I'm just a failure, aren't I? No job. No money. No home. Me wife doesn't wanna know. And now me daughter doesn't wanna know. It wouldn't be so bad if I could just see her."

But Lindsey hadn't even answered his letter.

Sinbad made comforting noises. What else could he do?

Quite a lot, it seemed. A few days later, Sinbad got into a funny mood. He went on an orgy of housework, clearing away Jimmy's bits of knock off and getting out the hoover for the first time ever. Jimmy had to go for a mid-week bath, much to his disgust.

There was a knock at the door. So that's what it was. A new bird for Sinbad. Except that when a smart young woman with dark curly hair stepped into the room, Jimmy realised she'd come for him. It was Lindsey. Sinbad had persuaded her to visit her poor, fed-up father. He hardly recognised her after six years, but she was still his little girl.

Sinbad brought in tea on a tray, then made himself scarce. Father and daughter didn't know how to start talking to each other. Jimmy's hands were shaking so much he spilt the tea. He couldn't believe how beautiful she'd got. She made the best of herself too, dressed in a black suit with a sharp red collar. Her make-up was as perfect as the girls on the beauty counter in Boots. For the first time, Jimmy was embarrassed by his room's downtrodden look. Stripes and flowers on the wallpaper and flock curtains.

Lindsey told him about her fiancé, Gary. He sounded like the kind of fella to delight any father. Good steady job working for a building society. They were planning the full works for the wedding, three bridesmaids, white roller and a reception at the masonic hall. As he listened to Lindsey chatting away and relaxing, Jimmy started to cheer up. He could picture himself in a top hat, linking arms with the blushing bride and posing for the photographer.

He was happier still when Lindsey called back two days later. She'd brought him a card for Father's Day. The first he'd had for years. It must be a sign that he was back in the family.

This time they talked about the past. Jimmy's good mood evaporated as Lindsey listed his faults one by one. What was worse was she didn't sound angry, just hurt. How had it happened? His excuses sounded pathetic as soon as they were out of his mouth. OK, so he'd been a bit of a lad, but he'd never meant to hurt anyone. He'd always tried to do things for the best.

"You weren't even bothered about me when you were at home."

The accusation cut Jimmy to the quick. "I was busy," he replied.

"You weren't bothered about me mother either," she continued. "All I can remember is you going in her purse for beer money."

"Yeah, well. It was for the horses."

"You promising us the earth when you got your big winner."

"I've changed."

"I'm trying to believe you. I used to think that some day we'd have a nice house, that me mum wouldn't always be worried about money. I don't want Gary and me to end up like you and me mum did."

Jimmy hadn't wanted to end up like his dad, but it seemed he had. He didn't know how he had got there.

There was more bad news. Far from handing over an invitation, Lindsey had come round to tell her own father not to come. She wanted that Ken Summers to give her away.

"He's been a much better dad to me than you. At least he's been around."

Now that she'd started, Lindsey was relentless. As usual, no one would give Jimmy a chance.

"Your mother wouldn't let me near the place," he said.

"You could have taken us out. Gary's mum and dad are separated, but his dad used to take them out."

"Where could I have taken you?"

"Oh, Dad. You've no idea, have you?" Lindsey sounded near to tears.

The worst thing was she was right. It never occurred to him to join the ranks of weekend fathers in the park. They were his kids. He'd thought that nothing could change that. Family was family. Didn't Lindsey's visit prove that? Weren't they making a fresh start?

"It's a bit too late for that."

"I'll change, love. I have changed. Honest."

"Look, Dad. I hardly know you."

"We can get to know each other, can't we? I'll see you at the wedding. I mean, I don't need to make a big speech or anything. I'll sit at the back if you want."

"Dad. You're not invited."

"Listen. It's different now we've met each other, isn't it? I promise you. I won't have anything to do with your mam or Ken. Honest. I won't even touch a drop. "

"This wedding's the biggest day of my life. I don't want things to go wrong. Keep away, will you. For my sake."

Jimmy brooded over what to do next. He'd wake up in the morning depressed as hell, hungover and feeling like the lowest of the low. Until he'd had his first bevvy, he was ready to crawl into a hole and die quietly, but as he drank he got his confidence back. By closing time he was ready to storm the church, defeat Ken in single combat and take his rightful place by his daughter's side.

The day before the wedding, he got a visit from Jackie. She stood in the middle of his room, despising it.

"I always knew you'd end up like this," she said so bitterly her spit would have burnt holes in the carpet. "Where are you planning to move to next, then? Walton or Strangeways?"

She'd come round for the sole purpose of making sure Jimmy kept away. It seemed Lindsey was worrying that her father might show up and ruin things.

"I don't want your dark shadow and bad smell hanging over us," Jackie went went on. "And our Lindsey wants peace of mind on her wedding day."

How dare she? As if he'd do anything to harm his little girl. "Tell her she's got nothing to worry about from me," he said. If he did turn up, he wouldn't cause any trouble.

It was as if Jackie could read his mind. "I want to tell her that you won't go anywhere near that wedding or that reception."

Jimmy nodded. He didn't have any choice.

"I want you to say it."

Bloody cow. Bitch. Humiliating him like that. "Alright," he said through gritted teeth. "You've done your job. You've made me feel as bad as I could ever feel. You tell our Lindsey I won't do anything to spoil her day."

He spent the night going over and over what he should do. No way could he leave it. His own daughter's wedding. In the end, he decided to turn up all posh, sneak into the reception and get thoroughly bladdered. That'd show them. While his suit was down the two-hour cleaners, he showered and shaved. He could have dined at the Ritz when he'd finished.

The service was at three o'clock. Jimmy got to the church at a quarter to. Hundreds of people in their glad rags and picture hats were milling about. As he got closer, he noticed they were smart. Really smart, with well cut suits and Italian shoes. Gary's family, of course. No-one was there from Lindsey's side. Who was there to invite? Jackie and that Ken would still be at theirs. Jimmy could just make out his son standing by the church door, dressed in the full gear and handing out service sheets.

Jimmy's nerve failed. He didn't belong with this lot. His suit had fitted in the seventies, but that was a long while ago. It wouldn't take a row for him to show Lindsey up. Just being there, standing out among these people, would be enough. Instead, he watched from the other side of the road.

A white roller pulled up. Jackie stepped out and posed for the photographer. She could have been in *Hello* magazine, she had that much class. The three little bridesmaids had arrived with her. They were in billows of pink taffeta, which frothed up as they jumped about and giggled.

The roller purred away to fetch the bride. The guests wandered into church and for a few minutes Jimmy was left alone. Then the car was back. Ken got out first to help Lindsey with her dress. It was a sea of white with a train that went on forever. Exactly what Jimmy would have picked for her. Her dark hair and a bouquet of deep red flowers were the only splashes of colour.

As she got out, Lindsey gave Ken a hug. They stayed like that till the photographer made them stand by the car for a picture. Jackie came up to give her daughter, their daughter, a kiss. She made sure the bridesmaids were in place before going into the church. Lindsey, on Ken's arm and flanked by pretty little girls, processed through the lich-gate and up to the church. From where he was, Jimmy heard the organ strike up the wedding march. The heavy oak doors closed behind his daughter and the only sound from the street was the dreary Saturday traffic.

Jimmy didn't wait for the ceremony to finish. His little girl was getting married and he couldn't ruin it for her, no matter how much she'd rejected him. He walked back to Sinbad's, feeling more alone than he ever had in his life.

Chapter 6

Jimmy 'Never Say Die' Corkhill wasn't ready to give up quite yet. He'd make something of himself, show them all. Dodgy deals and stupid scams weren't enough for him now. He was going after the bigger stuff. Frankie's name was still good for a few contacts. Someone put him on to someone who put him on to a woollie called Vinny. If Jimmy could come up with the goods, Vinny would get rid of them.

His first target was a post office, well away from Brookside Close. No weapons, nothing too hard. It worked. The clerk was so short he could barely see over the counter. One look at Jimmy, six foot tall and acting fierce, and he handed over the cash like a lamb. It was so easy Jimmy almost felt sorry for him. Until he counted the cash. Two hundred quid. Just like that.

Sinbad didn't believe Jimmy had it in him. So he had to prove it, didn't he? One briefcase whipped from an unlocked car. Dead smart and complete with mobile phone. The owner deserved to lose it. Soft lad Sinbad was breathless with shock, his little legs going nineteen to the dozen to keep up with Jimmy. It was the beer belly let him down. By contrast, Jimmy was fit for anything.

"I'm looking after meself from now on," he told his fat friend. "No one else will."

A bloke on a motor bike, no names, no questions, helped him with the next job. With Jimmy on the back, he swooped into a high street and paused outside a jeweller's. Jimmy lobbed a brick through the window, hopped off and helped himself. Meanwhile, the bike had done a circuit and they were off. It was five minutes of pure heaven. The thrill of getting away with it was the best thing Jimmy had felt for years.

Vinny came over to the flat. He was younger than Jimmy expected, with dyed blonde hair, a chain round his neck and a chunky signet ring on his pinky. He looked almost soft, till you saw the jagged scar running the length of his left cheek. Jimmy instinctively put his hand to the place where his hair was escaping from his forehead. The youth reminded him of the need to get somewhere fast.

The flat was full of Jimmy's stash. It was a lot classier than usual. The stones from the jewellers went down a treat. Vinny examined them carefully, and their new owner.

They were all getting on great, till Sinbad got back. Talk about ruining your image. He trotted in with that worried look on his face, wanting to know what was going on, refusing to back off. Jimmy had to bundle him out of the room. He knew there would be a row later, but he could handle Sinbad.

Sure enough, when Vinny had left Sinbad started moaning. Jimmy hadn't got time for any of that. He was on his way up. Finally, he was going to change his life. For the better.

"I'm going right to the top of the first division," he told Sinbad.

"Walton's Reserves, you mean, don't you? How do you like their kit? White with little arrows on it."

"You could worry for England, do you know that?"

"I've got nothing to worry about, have I? Just because I

share a flat with some divvy who thinks he can rob his way to the stars and uses my flat for his stash."

"So what are you saying? Do you want me to move out? Is that what you're saying?" Jimmy could risk it. He didn't need Sinbad any more. They were in different leagues now.

"No, I don't want you to move out." Sinbad sounded exasperated. "It's just all this robbing. It's got you on some sort of a high, a fix, like you're on drugs or something."

It was true. "And you want to know why? Because I'm going somewhere," Jimmy explained. "For once in my life, I'm on a roll. You wanna know why? Well, I'll tell you. Because I've cracked it. It was dead simple. If you think you're a loser, you are. All it takes is to think that you're something. That's the knack. Now I've sussed it, I can't go wrong."

The new Jimmy treated himself to a new watch and some smart clothes. All that settling down stuff hadn't worked. Kathy and Jackie had both let him down, so he wasn't going to bother with tarts any more.

Vinny invited him up to Newcastle to meet the big boys. He was recruiting for a major project. His manner was so bland, Jimmy almost missed his meaning.

"I'm in, Deffo?" he asked, trying to keep the excitement out of his voice.

"Like I said, they were impressed," growled the Mancunian.

A few days later, Jimmy was summoned to a meet in the park. He was so nervous he popped into The British Lion first for a swift pint. No problem. The clearing Vinny had told him about was deserted. Jimmy sat on a bench to wait.

"You were supposed to be here twenty minutes ago." Vinny came up behind him. His hand came down heavy on Jimmy's shoulder, his ring catching the light.

"Sorry." Despite the alcohol, Jimmy's heart was going like he was in a marathon. He didn't dare look round.

"You'll be more than sorry if you're late for a job," Vinny said.

"I'm still not sure about you, Corkhill. I'm not sure you've got it. Unless it's out of a whiskey bottle, and I'm not having that."

"I had a pint on the way down," Jimmy protested. He wasn't a drunk.

"What for? To calm your nerves?"

"Behave. What have I got to be nervous about?"

"It's going to be violent. Broken heads. Pick handles. Shot guns even."

"Don't frighten yourself, Vin." Jimmy was fine again. It was Vinny and his friend that scared him, not the work they were offering.

It took a bit to convince Vinny that Jimmy was sound, but eventually he was in. They were going to rob a night club. No ordinary night club, either. The owners had dozens of clubs and restaurants throughout Manchester. The profits were high and they objected to handing them over to the tax man, so every month they met at The Pink Flamingo to gather in the cash. Vinny reckoned Jimmy was in for a share of £100,000.

They needed two drivers and two robbers for the job. Jimmy was to be a driver. It wasn't worth mentioning to Vinny that he hadn't actually passed his test. He could handle a car well enough. His job was to wait outside the club, while his partner was in there gathering up the dosh. Vinny would be in the other car.

The night before the big one, Vinny brought Jimmy's partner to meet him. As he climbed into the car, Jimmy couldn't see the man's face. It was only when he looked in the rear-view mirror that he saw Joey Godden's ugly mug leering at him from the back seat. Of all people.

There was no question of bygones and the past between them. The bad blood was still fresh and flowing.

"I'll have your brother, just like I had your cousin. And your Frankie."

"Don't even dare mention his name."

"Frankie," Joey said immediately. "You always did get him to fight your battles for you, didn't you? It cost me ten years inside. I'm not going to forget that, sunshine."

Vinny told them to save the fighting till it was all over.

Joey started up again the next night, while they were waiting for the action to start. Jimmy kept his cool as far as he could. Joey was proving how stupid he was, winding up the fella who was responsible for getting him out.

"This might be your last job," said Godden, pulling a balaclava over his head.

"Shut it, will you?" muttered Jimmy.

"You could buy a one-way ticket down south, follow your big brother Billy. You better start running when this is all over. I'll have you, Corkhill."

With that, Joey got out of the car and followed Vinny into the club. While he was waiting, Jimmy thought about what he was going to do. Godden would be after him, Barry or no Barry. All the memories of Frankie dying, Mam crying over his grave, Billy scared south came flooding back, like he was drowning. The longing for revenge, to see Joey suffer as he and his family had suffered, was so powerful, Jimmy could hardly hold the steering wheel. He couldn't move. He had to stay where he was and wait for that murderer.

Suddenly there was an eruption from the club. A figure emerged and ran for the cars. There was a pause and the second came out, followed closely by a group of bouncers, shouting and giving chase. Vinny got to his car and was away. The seconds ticked past. Jimmy looked over his shoulder to see what was happening. Joey was slow, too slow, weighed down by a hundred thousand pounds in a leather bag. The bouncers had stopped running. One of them lifted something to his shoulder. A second did the same. Jimmy saw the gleam of gun barrels. Then he heard shots.

Godden was still running. He appeared at the side window, yelling at Jimmy to open the door. It seemed as though time stopped. For a brief moment, there was no noise, no yelling, no rain, no car. Only a choice. There's the handle. If it's turned, Joey's in the car and Jimmy gets his money. There's the lock. If it's pushed down, Joey dies and Jimmy gets his revenge.

Jimmy leaned across – and pushed down the lock. For a few seconds, Godden hammered on the window, screaming in terror. There was another shot and his face slammed, distorted, against the glass. Jimmy watched in horror as his enemy slid down the door, leaving a trail of blood. Then his foot pressed the accelerator and he was away.

Revenge wasn't sweet. Jimmy spent the next few days in a state of terror. He didn't dare go out, not even to the boozer. Rod let him stay at the Close, but made it clear it was for a week at the most. After that, Jimmy was on his own. Every time he heard the milkman, he practically threw up with fear.

The worst thing was having no one to talk to. He could hardly tell Rod what was going on. Besides, Rod was planning to get married. Diana took up most of his spare time.

As he lay awake at night Jimmy found his thoughts turning to Jackie. He'd always been able to tell her everything. She understood him like no one else ever had. Not even Kathy. It tormented him that he'd thrown away his marriage, let his perfect woman slip through his fingers.

Vinny or no Vinny, Jimmy had to get out. He managed to get to Jackie's without seeing a soul. He found her in the living room, making curtains for their Lindsey. She wasn't exactly overjoyed to see him, but when she saw what a state he was in she let him pour his heart out. He told her the whole sorry story. How he'd let a fella die so he could get his revenge.

"Who was it, Jimmy?" Jackie asked.

"The fella I always said I'd get."

"The fella who killed your Frankie?"

"Yeah. Only it wasn't like what I expected." No triumph. No satisfaction. Just a constant sick feeling.

Jackie bit off the thread. "You know, I hated Frankie," she said. "If he ever gave a fag to a woman, he always lit it for her first, as if to say, 'Remember, all things come from me'. Any woman. Even women he hardly knew."

Jimmy was astonished. He'd always thought Frankie could have had any bird he wanted – including Jackie. So she really had been his. He hadn't come second best to his big brother.

"I looked up to you, Jimmy," said Jackie. "Just for a few years. Till it all started to go wrong."

Was it a good or a bad meeting? On the one hand, they were cautiously friendly again. On the other, it highlighted what a mess Jimmy had made of his life.

The latter was even clearer when Vinny finally caught up with him. It was inevitable. A ring at the front door. Jimmy legs it round the back, to find Vinny waiting for him.

Vinny wasn't pleased, of course, but he wasn't after Jimmy's blood. He accepted Jimmy's story that Joey Godden hadn't reached the car by the time he was shot. Godden hadn't died, although he'd be paralysed for life. The message was that Jimmy Corkhill was a liability. He'd never work again, not even with his usual small-time fences. That was all Vinny had come round to say. Stay out of it.

There was a warning, of course. Vinny lit a match and held it to Jimmy's face. He dropped it on to the carpet, where it fizzled for a second and burnt out, leaving a small brown patch.

"Sorry I've made a little mark," he said. "I hope you get the message. I'd hate to have to mark your face."

That was it. End of story. No beatings. No retaliation. No more looking over his shoulder. Instead of being floored at losing all his contacts in one go, Jimmy found he felt nothing but relief.

Chapter 7

There was nothing for it. Jimmy Corkhill was going to have to go straight. At least, for a while. Vinny's message proved only too true. Cautiously, Jimmy tried to get rid of a few watches, nothing too valuable, but it proved impossible. "Can't help you there," came the reply, or "not my kind of thing" or, more directly, "after your last little outing . . .". Hopeless.

A place to lay the old weary head was becoming a problem too. He'd outstayed his welcome chez Rod and the thought of going back to Sinbad's gaff made him even more depressed. If Sinbad would let him stay.

Jimmy tried to tell himself that something would turn up, but his optimism was running out. He should have had more faith. Barry Grant, of all people, threw him a lifeline. He was building up the shops on Brookside Parade and needed a caretaker. It wasn't a difficult job, keeping a general eye out and pulling a few weeds from the flower beds. On the other hand, it wasn't well paid. Barry said he couldn't afford more than the odd tenner. What he could offer, however, was a flat. A nice cosy little number over the video shop. With money from the dole, Jimmy could manage well enough for the moment. It would give him a chance to get his act together.

The biggest problem was the loneliness. He wasn't exactly

flavour of the month down The Swan. If anyone did talk to him, it was usually to make some snide remark about his lack of bottle or driving skills. The British Lion was worse. When he finally plucked up the courage to venture down there, a heavy silence smothered the noise of conversation as soon as he opened the door. He stood for five minutes at the bar, while the landlord polished glasses and his barmaid flirted with a sales rep, before giving up.

Some days, the only person he talked to was Ron Dixon, who ran the Trading Post. Jimmy bought all his shopping there, just so he could pass the time of day, even though the prices were twice what they were in the supermarket. His evenings were a dreary routine of frozen pizzas, canned beer and the telly. There was never anything interesting on. Most of the time, Jimmy sat in front of a flickering screen, watching anonymous people doing meaningless things and brooding.

He wanted to go and see Jackie again, but didn't have the nerve. What excuse could he use? She'd got herself a decent man now, one with a nice little business. He had to admit Ken looked after her. If only he'd had the sense to do the same. If only he'd been there. If only they hadn't rowed. Round and round in his head, hour after hour. He'd been too busy being the hard nut. Jimmy the Sky. Too busy to notice he'd chucked away what some people are never lucky enough to have.

And there, in the centre of his brain, were two ominous, glowing figures. Four. Zero. Forty years old and what had he got to show for it? Mid life crisis? His life had been nothing but crises since the day he was born.

Two days before his birthday, Jimmy had a surprise visitor.

His son showed up in the Parade. At first, he was delighted. Jimmy Junior was growing up, tall like his father, and dark. Same taste in leather jackets as well. The spots would go when he was a bit older.

This was no friendly visit. In fact, Jimmy couldn't work out what was going on. The boy had a strange way of half saying things. His excuse for being there was that he was just passing. He wouldn't accept a drink off his old man. It seemed the only reason he'd come was to have a go at Jimmy.

"You two splitting up was the best thing that ever happened to me and me mum," he said as he left. It was the only complete sentence he'd uttered.

No-one remembered Jimmy's birthday. He wasn't surprised, but that didn't stop him from being disappointed. Thirteenth of November. Unlucky for some. Especially him. Definitely nothing to celebrate. He spent the afternoon on a bench in the Parade. It was freezing. Something about the cold appealed to Jimmy's mood.

He was roused from his sulks by the sound of heels on concrete. Jackie was striding her way across the pavement. Talk about a sight for sore eyes. Her tight bum and long legs looked as wonderful as ever in jeans and she could walk on a rockery with never a wobble.

"Here," she said, pushing an envelope into Jimmy's hands. For a moment, he thought fate had really done the dirty and delivered divorce papers to him on his birthday. But it was a card, with embossed flowers on. One of the pricier of Ron's collection. Inside she'd written: 'To Jimmy, with love, Jackie'. With love, eh. Perhaps things were looking up.

Jackie sat down on the bench, leaving a careful foot between them. They talked as if they were picking their way through a mine field. A word wrong and there would be an explosion. Lindsey, doing well and being happy, was a safe path. Then, casually, as if it was of no importance, Jackie dropped the bombshell.

She and Ken had split up.

"Sorry to hear it," Jimmy lied. He looked across at his wife, but she kept her eyes front and wouldn't glance back at him.

To break the silence, Jimmy mentioned their son. It was a dangerous topic, but it seemed to bring them together. Jackie thought Jimmy Junior was far too angry with his father ever to forgive him. She wondered why he'd suddenly turned against Jimmy like that. There seemed to be no reason for it. Only an afternoon of sordid passion with your sister, thought Jimmy, wincing as the guilt hit him.

The ice was definitely broken, though. The chill in the air was now entirely due to the weather. For the first time in weeks, Jimmy's spirits were on the way up. Perhaps going straight was the answer. Jackie would approve. Maybe he was in with a chance.

"If I ever get meself sorted out, I'll come back to you, you know," he said. He meant to sound super cool and confident, but his voice was still hesitant from lack of use.

"I won't hold me breath." Her mouth, in profile, lifted in a half sarcastic, half amused smile.

It was such a typical Jackie comment, Jimmy could have leaned over and kissed her. Not yet, though. He'd have to prove himself. Rub out the past somehow.

"I've gone straight, love. Honest. No choice, really. I was crap at the other."

That made her turn her head towards him at last. She was

laughing at him, like she used to. There was hope. He could still make her laugh.

Instead of brooding that night, Jimmy got down to some serious planning. He had to make up for the first forty miserable years of his life. Time to put right some of the mistakes. His job as a caretaker was alright, but he needed something to bring in a proper wage.

The answer came to him when he saw Ron Dixon tearing his hair out the next day. As well as the Trading Post, Ron had a mobile grocery van, known as the Moby. He'd had the Ford Transit painted blue with a picture of a whale on the side panel. It was a nice little earner, but Ron was chasing his tail trying to make regular deliveries and keep the shop going.

Enter Jimmy Corkhill, answer to all his prayers. Ron could sublet the Moby to him. He could get rent and make a bit on supplies. In return, Jimmy could take the profit. Since he had the time, he could expand the round. Reach the OAPs and housewives who had trouble getting into town. A perfect solution.

Ron took a bit of persuading, as he'd heard about Jimmy's reputation. In the end, he agreed as long as the rent was paid. Jimmy swore he'd be reliable. And he meant it. This time he'd changed for good. He had to if he was going to win Jackie back.

"What have you done to yourself?" she said when she saw him. He'd driven round there on his first day out.

"And I did it all for you." It was true. He'd actually gone into an ordinary shop and bought a set of white overalls. He reckoned he looked the part.

"Done what? What have you come as?" She was laughing at his special food handler's cap.

He showed her round. She took in the neat shelves of tins, the thermos of tea, the fridge for dairy products.

"I took on board what you told me the other day, you know, about getting meself sorted and that. Getting a proper job," he told her. "This is just the start, kiddo."

"I'm surprised it can manage to. Start, I mean."

"Hey, don't mock this. It can do 35 downhill with a following wind. If you wind the lacky band up to start with."

"Not much use for a fast getaway, though, is it?"

"Don't think I'll be making any, do I?"

"Yeah. We'll see."

They shared the tea, taking turns at sipping from the plastic mug. Jimmy was desperate to convince her this was legit, not some fly-by-night scam. Since he'd heard Ken was off the scene, he'd been dreaming of getting back together with her. He told her about the nights lying awake, cursing himself for his stupidity. All he wanted was another chance.

"It's not that easy," she said. "You can't just walk in and take it all back, Jimmy."

"I know that. I don't expect it." Although he had half hoped. "I know I've gotta prove meself to you and that. But look. All this. This is it, isn't it, eh? Go on. Admit it. You are just a bit impressed, aren't you?"

"Yeah I am," she grinned. "A bit."

The campaign began in earnest. It was made a lot easier when Ron offered Jackie a job at the Trading Post. From behind the counter she could see Jimmy making good. Persistence won her over in the old days, it would work again.

The Moby was doing well. Jimmy wouldn't charge over the odds to the old dears. If anyone knew what it was like to be short of the readies, it was him. Quantity was what he was after. It worked, too. He was making money offering a good service. Everyone was happy.

November ticked over to December. Jimmy watched Jackie joking with the customers. Their wedding anniversary was the next day. Twenty years ago, 2nd December 1971, they'd married. On an impulse, he stowed the van and went into town. In C & A's he found a turquoise dress, low cut with frills in all the right places. Jackie'd look a treat in it. He planned to take her out somewhere special. There was a great Chinese restaurant just opened.

Ron had got into the Christmas spirit. You couldn't see the shelves for paper streamers. Jackie was decorated too, with a garland of purple tinsel in her hair. Jimmy felt as embarrassed as a schoolboy asking for a date.

"Listen, Jack. Er – I was wondering. How do you fancy a night out?" he asked.

"If I knew it was going to have this effect, I'd have put tinsel in me hair years ago," she replied.

He brought out the dress and convinced her it was legit. She looked inside the bag and laughed.

"Well, you do me ego a lot of good," she said. "I haven't been a size 8 for a long time."

As far as Jimmy was concerned, she looked the same as she had twenty years ago.

The meal was wonderful. Even the food was good. Jackie changed the dress and got a stunner in pink with tiny boot-lace straps. Perhaps it was more her style. She always did have good taste.

"What are we celebrating?" she asked as the waiter opened a bottle of genuine champagne.

"Cast your mind back to another celebration," said

57

Jimmy. "Another posh frock. A white one. Twenty years ago today, Jack, you and me walked up that aisle."

"December 2nd, 1971." She took a sip from her glass. "Pity you didn't have such a good memory when we were together."

"That's a bit harsh, isn't it? I'm making up for it now, aren't I?"

It seemed he was. That evening they started courting all over again.

Chapter 8

Lindsey was gossiping with Jackie in the Trading Post. Jimmy could tell something was up as soon as he went in.

Jackie greeted him with "Hiya, Grandad."

"Hey. Less of the grandad, you," said Jimmy. "I'm still in my prime, you know. What's going on?"

"Have you told him?" said Lindsey.

"Who? Grandad?" asked Jackie.

Jimmy was mystified. "Told me what? Will somebody tell me what's going on."

Lindsey was beaming. "Gran-dad," she whispered in a shy sing-song.

At last he got it. He gave Lindsey an enormous hug. Then he hugged Jackie, then they all hugged each other.

"We're made up for you, aren't we, Jack?" His voice wobbled with happiness. Jackie nodded. She was with him. They were proud parents awaiting their first grandchild. Together.

For the first time, Jimmy had a real purpose in life. Once he and Jackie were back together, everything would be great. He'd do it properly this time. No messing about. No more lies. No more broken promises. They'd be a family. He had to convince her that this time he really meant it.

Going out together was great. The magic was still there. He could make her smile. She could turn him on. The problem was the serious stuff, the mundane duties of washing up and paying the rent. Jimmy plucked up the courage to ask Jackie if he could move back in with her.

"What do I have to do to prove how much I love you?" he begged. "I'm holding down two jobs. I want to live with you again. I want us to be a proper married couple again, especially now we're going to be grandparents for the first time."

"You want a lot, don't you?"

"I just want to make it up to you for letting you down, that's all."

If she couldn't hear the sincerity in his voice then, she never would. She said she'd think about it, so he went on the attack, pestering her with good times and reminiscences. Joking and laughing and playing the fool, like he used to. But unlike the old days, he was there every day with the Moby. And he was the perfect caretaker, the flats were guarded and the flower beds spotless.

To his astonishment, not only did Jackie like him better every day, he was starting to like himself. He actually enjoyed going out and selling things. As well as the chat there was the freedom of being more or less his own boss. At night, he dreamed again of a house of his own. He added a shop. A little business, nothing too grand, but enough to keep them in their old age. He dreamed of growing old with Jackie, surrounded by grandchildren and soft furnishings.

"Alright. I've made me mind up. I'll let you move back in," Jackie said. It was almost out of the blue. They were in the Trading Post, like any other morning.

Jimmy could hardly believe what he'd just heard. "Come on. I'm serious," he said.

"So am I. What more do you want?"

Jimmy was overjoyed. "I want you to believe I'm a changed man. And that I'll never let you down again."

"I must be off me head, but I'll give you one more chance. One more, Jimmy, and that's it. Don't ever let me down again."

He knew he never would. This time it was for real. They smooched in full view of the customers. Jimmy wanted the world to know that he was in love with his wife.

Moving day came. Jimmy's worldly goods were piled up on the pavement, ready to be loaded into the Moby. One trip should do it. Jimmy looked round to find Jimmy Junior watching him.

"What are you doing round here? Your mam sent you?" Jimmy had a feeling this was no friendly visit. Junior was standing with his arms folded, just out of reach.

"No."

"Come to give us a hand?"

"No."

"Can you run to anything else, besides 'no'?" Uneasiness made Jimmy belligerent. "I mean, is 'yes' too exhausting for you? Still, I live in hope. Families and that. Getting back together again."

"So what makes you think you're coming back then?"

"Your mum and me – it's wrong isn't it. We're a family. We should be together."

"Family? When were you ever family?" Jimmy Junior almost spat the words out. "You don't know the meaning of the word."

"I've apologised for that, haven't I?" If Jackie could forgive him, Jimmy Junior could as well.

"Look, me and me mum were doing fine without you.

We've managed for long enough. We don't need you messing things up again."

"Is that all you've got to say?"

"No. I've got a message for you as well. It's quite simple. Even you'll understand. If you move back into our life, I'll tell me ma about the time I came home from school early." He put on a scared little boy's voice. "It was horrible. Me dad and Auntie Val thrashing around on the carpet with no clothes on. Me dad's kecks round his ankles. Auntie Val with her bits hanging out. What were they doing?"

Jimmy knew he meant it. His own flesh and blood threatening him. If Jackie found out about that one time with Val she'd never forgive him. It was so unfair. The one time he'd been unfaithful – apart from Kathy and that was different. Val had used him. Caught him in a moment of weakness. It wasn't his fault. He was only human, wasn't he?

Perhaps the best thing would be to put the move off until Jimmy Junior had calmed down. He could say he had to stay in the flat because he was the caretaker. That was it. She wouldn't want him to lose his job.

Jackie didn't buy it. "Oh, that's typical. I might have guessed. One week of responsibility and you're out of there so fast you couldn't catch you on Concorde. I knew you'd do this to me. I knew it."

"I've told you. It's me job, isn't it?"

"What job? Your job is on the Moby. The other is just a favour you were doing in return for free accommodation and the odd tenner. Barry Grant will just have to find some other caretaker, because you won't be needing the flat any more if you move in with us."

There was nothing for it. His only chance was to tell Jackie first and beg her forgiveness, before Junior piped up. The big day was the following Friday. Jimmy arranged to bring the Moby, complete with the rest of his gear, round to the Trading Post after the week's cashing up had been done.

All day the van had rattled with his worldly goods, black bin bags sliding across the floor every time he turned a corner. He couldn't concentrate for worrying about how he should confess. His customers kept asking him if he was alright. Two of them complained he'd short changed them and god knows how many got away with a bit extra.

He finished the round dead on time and headed for the Parade. Taking it carefully, he turned into Denham Street, hugging the kerb instead of cutting the corner as usual. As he went round, he realised he was too close. There was the sound of tyres scraping on concrete and an ominous hiss.

Cursing his bad luck, Jimmy hopped out of the Moby to see the damage. A flat. A real honest-to-god flat. Why did it always happen to him? Anyone else would have got away with a slow puncture. Jimmy wasn't bad at mechanics, but it still took him half an hour to change the wheel.

Jackie was furious when he finally showed up. She wouldn't believe what had happened.

"And you saw this spaceship hovering over the dock road and a strange voice says to you . . ." she said sarcastically when he tried to tell her about the flat.

"Hang on. Look at this." Jimmy held out his hands, covered in oil and grime. "Proof."

Jackie inspected them. "A real puncture?" she said doubtfully.

"A real puncture," Jimmy confirmed. "In this real van. Look, it's going to be what it should have been and never was.

Truth. Trust." He took a deep breath and started to tell her about Val.

Jackie cut him short. "Is this a confession?" she said. "I don't think I want to hear it. Not tonight."

Junior chose that moment to make his entrance.

"What are you doing here?" Jackie asked.

He stared at Jimmy, and chose his words carefully.

"I've been waiting round the back for you, Jimmy. I warned you, didn't I? What I'd do if you came back."

He was as good as his word. Ignoring Jimmy's pleas for just a moment alone with Jackie so he could explain, Jimmy Junior told the whole sorry tale.

"Those barmaids. That was nothing. I got used to that. But her own sister. Me Auntie Val. Lying on the carpet like a pair of dogs, you were. You can't forgive me, can you? For knowing what a lying toe rag you are," he finished.

Jackie's face was grey. She had retreated behind the counter, her head down as she heard the tale.

"I was going to tell you," Jimmy pleaded. "I still want you to have me back."

"My God, you've got some cheek," she said and wouldn't listen to Jimmy's side of the story.

The stupid thing was it had only been Val. The barmaids really had been nothing. Flirting helped the ale go down. Why did it have to be his wife's sister of all people? Why had Junior decided to come home early on that day of all days? It didn't matter how hard Jimmy tried, it seemed as if the odds were always against him.

So he went back to the flat. Back to being caretaker. Jackie would hardly speak to him. The wooing process would have to start all over again.

Strangely enough, Jimmy did have someone on his side. Lindsey was definitely pushing her parents together as much as her brother was pulling them apart. She told Jimmy to get his act together, wash, shave and go on the attack. He saw her talking to Jackie. From the looks on their faces, she was having a hard time persuading her mother to give him a chance.

Jimmy and Jackie talked. They laughed. He could always make her laugh. But the stumbling block was their son. He'd move out if Jimmy crossed the threshold. As far as Jimmy was concerned, that was fair enough, but Jackie saw it differently.

"How do you think he felt when he saw his dad making out with his Auntie Val?" she said. "Not only that, but he's kept it to himself all these years without telling anyone."

"I know. But I can't turn back the clock. It's done now."

There was a pause. Jackie had a funny little smile on her face. "I've known all along about you and our Val," she said quietly.

"You what?"

"She told me."

Jimmy couldn't believe his ears. "She *told* you? All these years and you never said?"

Suddenly Jackie was almost snarling. "I wouldn't give you the satisfaction to know how much it hurt." Abruptly, her mood changed again and she was teasing. "Anyway, she didn't rate you very much."

"How do you mean?"

"Out of ten. You got a four. It would have been less, but fractions were never her strong point."

Jimmy was ready to give up. He made one final speech.

"Look. I've changed." How many times had he said that?

"I've got a steady job and legit money in me pocket. I've gone straight now. I've had a taste of the wrong side and I can't hack it any more. I couldn't survive a police cell now. What more do you want? If you don't say yes, I'll walk out that door and I swear, Jackie, you'll never see me again."

He meant it too.

Doubtfully, hesitantly, as if each word gave her pain, Jackie agreed to give him one last final chance. When Jimmy Junior protested, she told him it was her life and he could like or lump it. It was no surprise that he chose to leave.

Jimmy was relieved. He wasn't proud of his son's hatred, but he couldn't do anything about it. The main thing was that he and Jackie were back together.

This time the move went off without a hitch. Jimmy's stuff fitted in perfectly. Like he'd never been away. As Jackie lay in his arms, sleeping peacefully where she belonged, he silently promised her that she'd never have any reason to throw him out again.

Chapter 9

For a while, things went spectacularly well. The Moby went from strength to strength. Jackie was enthusiastic, diversification was her idea. A few extra lines for sale, unbeknown to Ron, would go down a treat. She was right. It was getting to the stage where people would wait for the Moby to come round, even if they could get to the Trading Post easily.

Jimmy might have known it was too good to last. He and Jackie set up a stall outside a school. The little horrors had far too much money for sweets, but who was he to complain? The takings were so good he couldn't resist giving Jackie a big smacker as they were driving up to a set of traffic lights.

Which promptly turned red while Jimmy wasn't looking.

There was a horrible crunch as the Moby drove cheerfully into the car in front. Confession time once again. Jimmy hadn't quite got round to mentioning his lack of a licence to Jackie. Needless to say, she almost exploded with rage when she heard.

She sat fuming in the front as Jimmy gave Ron Dixon's name and details to the police and the bloke in the other car. It was the only way out. As they drove slowly home, he blocked out Jackie's whinging by thinking up ways to get hold of Ron's papers.

Jimmy spent the next week in a panic. The Moby was no

problem, he had a mate who could repair it cheap. Getting hold of the other man was more difficult. A yuppie type, who was never in. Jimmy got more and more edgy. He had money to pay him off, but if he didn't find him soon he'd have smoked the lot.

Fate, as ever, was against him. He didn't find the fella. The fella found him. Or rather, he found Ron Dixon. The real Ron Dixon, who was not exactly overjoyed by Jimmy's conduct. And that was the end of the Moby for Jim. Ron wouldn't listen to any explanations. In fact, he was thoroughly unreasonable about the whole thing.

One step forward, two step back. The story of his life. Aggrieved at life's unfairness, Jimmy went back to the dole queue. It was worse than usual. Before, he had always had a little something on the side to keep him going, a deal or a scam or two. Now there was nothing. Vinny's message was still being received loud and clear and all Jimmy got from his enquiries was a deafening silence.

No job. And soon no home either. Jimmy was convinced he'd blown it with Jackie. She would have been alright about him being made redundant, or something like that. Getting sacked for pulling a fast one was a different matter.

Jimmy slunk around the house for days, keeping out of the way. He was bored out of his skull. What Jackie let him have out of his dole money hardly bought a pint. He wasn't in a position to argue with her. Every time she opened her mouth, which wasn't often, he was terrified it was to tell him to get out.

There was nothing to do but brood. The worst thing was that he had been doing OK. The Moby was a nice little earner. Jimmy was good with customers. A bit of the old charm. Flirting with the women. Jokes for the kiddies. He'd actually been enjoying it. His first proper straight job and he blew it. On the scrap heap again. Older and wiser. Well, older. What was he fit for? Nothing.

At least he felt a bit more secure at home. As long as he kept up the appearance of trying to find work, Jackie seemed to tolerate his presence. What annoyed her was seeing him vegetate, so he went through the motions. Scoured the local papers. Asked around. The highlight of his day was going through all the exciting opportunities at the Job Centre. Employers were falling over themselves to take on a scally with no qualifications and a prison record. He couldn't even get an interview for MacDonalds.

He hardly had the bus fare into town, so he spent most of his afternoons mooching about on the Parade. Sinbad had taken over his job as caretaker, so there was usually somebody to pass the time of day. When Sinbad was on his window-cleaning round, Jimmy would sit on a bench, counting the customers. He'd make a game of it. Make bets with himself on which shop was doing best. The Trading Post irritated him by coming out on top most of the time. The Pizza Parlour was busy, even in the afternoons. The quietest was the video hire place. Not surprising, when you considered the crappy selection there was.

All in all, the rents must bring in a tidy amount. Barry Grant was obviously doing well. Who'd have thought he'd end up as an entrepreneur?

A little shop would do Jimmy. He knew what kind it'd be. One of those discount stores, with a permanent sale and everything half price. A shop for ordinary people to get extraordinary bargains. Not bad that. Perhaps he ought to go into advertising.

69

Shopper spotting got more comfortable by May. It was almost pleasant to sit outside watching the world go by. Jimmy was relaxing into unemployment. At the back of his mind was an irritation that he should be doing something, getting on, making his mark, but with half the population out of work there didn't seem to be much point.

Until the video store went bust overnight. A 'To Let' sign went up and the windows were whitewashed. Jimmy wondered if they'd done a bunk. Sinbad couldn't shed any light on the matter. A plan started to form in Jimmy's head. He persuaded Sinbad to lend him the keys. Just to have a look. Out of curiosity, like.

Sinbad handed the keys over, despite a few misgivings. He supposed it was alright, since Jimmy was a mate. Then he toddled off with his ladders, leaving Jimmy the master of all he surveyed.

The unit was the smallest on the parade. The perfect size for a discount store. And in the perfect location. The empty room echoed forlornly. All that was left was the counter. No problem. The stock could be piled up in bins and buckets. Putting up a few shelves would be a piece of piss. You didn't want anything too posh for a shop specialising in the cheap and cheerful. Behind the shop itself was a store room and a toilet. Nothing grand, but enough for what Jimmy wanted.

On the back of an old envelope he started to make some calculations. It wouldn't take much to compete with the Trading Post on price. Not that Jimmy would stock exactly the same stuff, but getting a dig at Ron Dixon would be an added bonus. He knew where to get the gear, too. All perfectly legit. There were still one or two people prepared to do him favours, provided he paid cash for them. The secret was in knowing where the bargains were to be had.

Overheads would have to be kept to a minimum. Jimmy wasn't exactly rolling in it. Rent could be a problem. Perhaps Barry would give him a discount or something. After all, they were family, sort of.

It worked out better than that. Barry disappeared. The rumour went around that he was dead. Jimmy was delighted. Barry wasn't his favourite human being and if he was out of the way, he couldn't make a fuss about someone squatting one of his shops.

Jimmy borrowed a bit here, begged a bit there and started stocking up. Sinbad clocked him unloading and asked the odd nosy question, but was only really concerned in case he got into trouble.

"No problem, mate. With Barry out the way, the coast's clear, isn't it?" Jimmy pointed out to him. "We are going to make a fortune."

The best part was Jackie's enthusiasm. At first she was worried about the rent, but seeing as Barry wasn't around to take it anyway, she shrugged her shoulders and got on with it. It was her idea to call the place 'Kowboy Kutz'.

"That's really you, that is," she said with a grin.

"Very funny, you," Jimmy replied. "Look. This is all legit. Honest. What've I got to do to convince you?"

"All right. I believe you. Thousands wouldn't."

Talk about give a dog a bad name, but she'd be laughing on the other side of her face when they were millionaires. He was building up his stock, something for everyone. There were plastic drainers and cutlery drawers for a quid, scourers a quarter the price of Brillo pads and packs of ten pens for what one cost next door. There were dust bins, safety pins, shopping bags, hand bags, bum bags, plain mugs, mugs with royalty on them – for only 50p extra – tea cups, tea pots and tea caddies (more pictures of the queen). In a dark corner, Jimmy tucked away a few fun items – leather thongs, saucy nighties and a little stand of cut-price condoms.

Everything was now ready for the grand opening. He got hold of some florescent signs: 'BARGAINS GALORE' and 'CHEAP AND CHEERFUL' in yellow, 'DISCOUNTS' in pink and 'HALF PRICE' in orange. No-one was going to miss them. Focal point of the Parade, they were.

The Dixons were worried. Jackie took opening day off from the Trading Post. She'd be able to give it up completely once Kowboy Kutz was established. DD had a quiet word about competition. Jimmy told her that he wasn't going to be selling the same stuff as Ron, so she'd no need to fear. It was more or less true. The only overlap was in biros and notepads, which Jimmy was offering with a 75% discount.

The shop was a roaring success. The first day was packed out. Ron Dixon wasn't too happy, but everyone else was. It was so good, Jimmy was in danger of running out of stock. Jackie didn't stop smiling from opening to closing time.

"Brilliant, eh?" Jimmy said as they locked up for the night. "You stick with me, girl. We're on the way up. First the shop, then the house. Wait and see."

"You and your dream house," said Jackie, but she was still smiling.

The rumours of Barry's death were just that, but he hadn't actually made it back to Liverpool. Apparently, he was doing some deal with some crowd in Birmingham. Which was great from Jimmy's point of view. He simply let it be known he'd sorted everything out with Barry and there was no one to contradict him.

The Corkhills were definitely going up in the world. Rod and Di were tying the knot. Jimmy was made up for them. Di was a great girl, pretty and quiet. Not over bright, but that wasn't a bad thing in a wife. Sometimes, much as he loved her, Jimmy found Jackie too bright by half.

Uncle Jimmy and Auntie Jackie did them proud. The reception was a barbecue in the garden and Jimmy got to make a speech. Everything was going well until Ron Dixon collared him about business. He mentioned rents and Jimmy immediately got the wind up. Ron said something about Barry putting a firm called Fletcher's in charge of collecting the money.

"Well it's only fair, isn't it?" said Jimmy.

"And what about the 20% they put on top?" Ron continued. "For collecting it, like?"

"Bit steep, isn't it?" As soon as he said it, Jimmy felt the ground disappear from under his feet. He tried to edge away. "I've got to mingle."

"You're squatting, you are." Ron's face had turned purple.

"Behave, will you, Ronnie?" Jimmy was quick with excuses. "Barry Grant is doing me a favour for once. I'm just keeping that unit alive for a while."

"Grantie wouldn't do anybody any favours. You're squatting, aren't you, Jimmy? Admit it."

Ron had a point, but Jimmy had a better one. "Can you imagine Barry Grant letting someone squat in one of his units? Don't be soft, Ronnie. I'll get you another drink."

Jimmy thought that was the end of it until he got a visit from another inhabitant of Brookside Close. Max Farnham was the golden boy of Fletcher's and everything Jimmy despised. Well dressed, well spoken, smooth and smarmy. You just had to look at him to think money. So it was with great pleasure that Jimmy told him to get lost.

"I've got a key, haven't I?" he said smugly. "There's nothing you can do about it. No forced entry. No criminal damage. In fact, I'm looking after the place."

"Right," Max said. "If that's the situation, I suppose there's nothing we can do about it. For the moment. But I wouldn't get too comfortable, if I was you."

Jimmy wasn't worried. He'd have something sorted by the time Fletcher's got a court order and bailiffs. Ron gave him nasty looks and snide comments, but there wasn't anything else he could do. Jimmy thought he was safe enough.

Two weeks later, his water and electricity were cut off.

Chapter 10

There was nothing for it but to carry on. Jimmy wasn't going to be defeated. Water wasn't too much of a problem. A couple of buckets saw to the toilet and he took a thermos and a few tinnies to ward off thirst. Light and heat took a bit more working out. Gas canisters proved to be the answer. It was high summer, so he didn't need a lot of fuel. By the time winter came round, he'd have worked something out.

The inconvenience was worth it just to see Ron's face. He was hopping mad. Jimmy saw him watching balefully as customers poured into Kowboy Kutz, while the Trading Post suffered a lull. Serve him right for trying to put the boot in. So he wasn't paying rent at the moment. Sinbad reported that Max had said Fletcher's probably wouldn't bother to do anything about it. All's fair in love, war and business.

There was a warm glow of family around Jimmy again. Rod and Di were doing well. Di got a job on a make-up counter. Dead smart and she didn't have to worry about reading and writing. Then Jimmy got a visit from a young fella in a suit. He introduced himself as Brian Kennedy and he'd just taken over the hairdressing salon on the parade. Did Jimmy know where to find Tracy Corkhill? No problem. In fact, Jimmy was delighted to oblige.

Tracy was sharing Julia Brogan's council house. Julia was

good at playing the doting grandmother, even if she was a pain in the proverbial to everyone else. Although she was a trained hairdresser, Tracy hadn't been able to find work for a while. When Brian offered her the post as manageress of the salon, she was delighted.

Jimmy was made up. The whole family was doing well. Rod and Diana were settling down. Tracy was becoming a career woman. Kowboy Kutz was raking it in. Best of all, Lindsey gave birth to a little girl, Kylie. Entrepreneur, favourite uncle, doting grandad. There was no end to the roles Jimmy could play. And every single one was on the level.

There was a kind of family feeling around the shops in the Parade as well. Even Ron simmered down. Since Jackie was still working for him, he could hardly stay angry forever. Besides, Kowboy Kutz really wasn't in the same market. They may as well all get on together.

Jimmy had a chance to prove his community spirit sooner than he expected. Mick Johnson, owner of the Pizza Parlour, had been having trouble with British National Party thugs. Jimmy was disgusted at the racism coming from his own neighbours. Mick was a good bloke, trying to make something of his life. He didn't deserve hassle just because of the colour of his skin. It wasn't just the young louts, either. There was an old bloke, George Webb working in the Pizza Parlour, and he was always shouting his mouth off about immigration and keeping to your own kind. Which proved what a load of shite it all was. Mick only had to open his mouth to prove where he came from. Liverpool. Born and bred.

Kowboy Kutz was doing so well Jimmy didn't have time to organise the stock while it was open. He was often the last person to lock up. One night, he spotted a couple of figures hanging around the Pizza Parlour. They were crouched low by the door. It looked like they were fixing something, Jimmy couldn't see what it was.

"Oy," he shouted. "What d'you think you're playing at?"

There was the sound of breaking glass, then the two scarpered. Even in the dark, Jimmy could tell they were both young with skinhead hair cuts. Probably wearing parkas. Nazi gits.

He gave chase, fuelled by sheer rage. How dare they invade? Despite their head start, Jimmy caught up with them. One got away, but he landed the other with a flying tackle. The boy was surprisingly light. Jimmy only needed one hand to slam him against the wall.

"Right, you," he said. "You're for it now."

As he swung his arm back, ready to punch, someone grabbed hold of it. It was George Webb, clinging on for dear life. They struggled for a moment, just long enough for the lad to escape. Jimmy rounded on George.

"What d'you go and do that for?" he asked furiously.

"I might ask you the same question." George was brimful of self-righteousness. "He was just a lad. Half your size. You're a bully. D'you know that?"

"Me? A bully?" Jimmy was open mouthed with the cheek of it. "That lad was getting ready to torch Mick's place."

They went back to the Pizza Parlour together. Sure enough, the smashing sound had been a milk bottle breaking. Shards of glass were scattered outside Mick's door, swimming in a pool of petrol. Crude, but effective.

Jimmy was the hero of the hour. Mick shook his hand so hard he almost dislocated his shoulder and promised him free pizzas for a month. Even Ron was willing to let bygones be bygones. As for Jackie, she couldn't get enough of him.

The only one who wasn't impressed was Barry Grant. He turned up out of the blue, the last person Jimmy wanted to see. Hardly renowned for being full of the milk of human kindness, Barry wasn't going to give Jimmy any brownie points. Hero or no hero.

Jackie and Jimmy went over their accounts. The rent was about £100 a week. They could just about manage that now.

"It'll be alright, love," Jackie said. For once, she was the optimist. Jimmy was worried. Barry Grant had no reason to want him for a tenant. He'd probably want him out.

Barry proved more reasonable than Jimmy expected, but he might as well have sent in the bailiffs straightaway. Paying the current bill was no problem. The sticking point was almost £2,000 back rent.

"I'd like to help you, Jim," Barry said. "But I can't let it go. It wouldn't be fair on my other tenants."

He looked Jimmy steadily in the eye, cool as glass. No hint of triumph, but Jimmy could feel it. Barry wouldn't do anybody any favours. Least of all a Corkhill. If Jimmy could find the money, fine. If not, he was out on his ear.

Back at Kowboy Kutz, Jimmy gazed at what he'd achieved. A thriving business, happy customers, proud wife. Hero status – for a while, at least. He was actually doing something. Making something of his life at long last. How could he lose it all for a measly two grand? It wasn't fair. He was doing his best, wasn't he? There had to be a way out.

Try as they might, he and Jackie couldn't think of one. They had no capital or assets. Nor had anyone else they knew. Rod and Di were pushed to find the mortgage money each month. Tracy had used up her savings while she was unemployed. No bank would touch them and Jackie wouldn't let Jimmy go to a loan shark.

Jackie tried talking to Barry. She could have saved her breath. He simply repeated that he wanted his money. End of story. Sinbad told them that he'd been given a hard time for giving Jimmy the key in the first place.

Barry wasn't going to give them any time to find a solution. He was back two days later to say that the matter was in the hands of his solicitor. Jimmy knew what that meant. The court. An order to pay. No money. The bailiffs. He got Sinbad to help him shift some of the stock. At least he'd have something to show for it.

He was back early the next morning to move the rest of his stuff. Only it wasn't there. Kowboy Kutz was a burnt-out ruin. Apparently there'd been an explosion about an hour after he and Sinbad had locked up. Whoever had done it probably hadn't realised there were gas canisters in the back. The place was wrecked. Sinbad was sweeping up glass from the whole length of the parade. The bricks were charred and the door was in pieces. Inside was worse. The store and toilet had been demolished. Where the counter had been, there was now a heap of burnt wood. Jimmy picked up one piece and put it on top of another. It wouldn't balance, clattering to the floor.

What was the point in clearing up? Everything was destroyed. Everything he'd worked for. This time he'd really tried to make a go of it and someone had just come along and ruined it. He stood there, in the middle of melted biros and drainers, and howled. The acrid smell of burnt plastic filled his nostrils. Red and yellow crates had turned from cheerful usefulness to ugly, misshapen pustules. Restless black soot, as black as his mood, covered every surface. It was stirred by the wind blowing through the jagged edges of the shop front. A bit of newspaper landed on Jimmy's sleeve. He brushed it off, but it stuck to his hand. The typeface was familiar. 'EW BRITA' ran along the top line. New Britain. He might have known. It was those bastard racists.

Outside, the rubber necks had gathered. Vultures. Giving his pain a wide berth, none of them would step inside to help or sympathise. Jimmy wandered out, not knowing what else to do. A path through the crowd opened up to let him pass. He could hear whispered speculations. Everyone loved a mystery. They were enjoying the shock horror of the situation.

"Alright, love?" Jackie was at his side, almost in tears herself.

Sinbad was there too, placing himself sleeve to sleeve with his friend. "Sorry, mate," he whispered.

Flanked by his two guardians, Jimmy made his way home to despair.

The afternoon wore on to evening and into night. He went over and over it with Jackie. She tried to put a brave face on it, but it was no use.

"You'll find something else, love," she said. She pressed his hand. "Look, I know how much that shop meant to you, but you've got to get over it. There'll be other chances."

Jimmy brought his lips together in a tight attempt at a smile. He pressed her hand till the knuckles whitened, but couldn't trust himself to speak. A grown man crying over a few bits of burnt plastic. It was pathetic. He was pathetic. His dream had gone up in smoke. Literally. God knows, he hadn't exactly gone for the moon. Was it too much to hope for? A shop and a house? What was wrong with him?

It hardly seemed worth the bother of getting up the next day. Jackie brought him breakfast in bed, but he was too depressed to enjoy the treat. Here she was, supportive, loving, everything a wife should be. What had he got to offer her? Nothing. He'd let her down again. It wasn't his fault. He'd tried the best he could, but he just couldn't hack it.

"I'm sorry, Jack," he told her over and over. "I didn't mean to."

"What'll you do now? Why don't you have a word with Barry? Maybe he'll let you start up again if you clear up the mess."

"No chance. Not worth me even asking." Jimmy couldn't face the thought of crawling to Barry Grant. "Why should he help me? He's got what he wanted. Kowboy Kutz is history."

Jackie took the tray with its plate of congealing bacon and cold fried eggs. Jimmy hadn't even been able to manage the coffee. She stood awkwardly in the doorway, something on her mind.

"Look, Jim, I know you've had a set back," she said tentatively. "But promise me you won't go back to the scams and the dodgy deals."

Jimmy shrugged. What else was he fit for? After Vinny, it probably wasn't even an option. A lifetime of the dole queue was rolling out before his very eyes.

"Promise me."

"I dunno, love. I don't want to, but what else am I gonna do? There's nothing else for me. I'm a failure. Everything I touch goes down the pan. I dunno. I'll see."

He could feel her disappointment in the pit of his stomach, but he couldn't think of anything else to say.

Chapter 11

Help came from the most surprising source. Of all people, Barry Grant offered him a job. He'd gone into the entertainments business and joined forces with a group called Halsall Leisure. Hence his disappearance a few months ago. He'd been forming a partnership with one Joe Halsall. Together they were going to set the suburbs of Liverpool alight. There was an empty cavern at the end of the Parade. Barry was going to transform it into the glitziest of glitzy nightclubs. By Christmas, La Luz would be welcoming in the young, the trendy and, above all, the big spenders.

Jimmy's job would be Director of Security. Barry was going to send him to Birmingham for a couple of weeks to learn the ropes in one of Halsall's mega nightclubs. After that, he'd have a guaranteed job in the new place.

Barry gave him a fistful of notes for expenses. There was enough for a DJ, plus the fare to Birmingham three times over. Jimmy decided to use the extra to give Jackie a treat. He bounced into the Trading Post to give her the glad tidings. Her reaction was less than thrilled. She'd seen Barry giving Jimmy money and was immediately suspicious. When she heard about his job title, she flipped.

"Director of security? A bouncer, you mean. Head and only bouncer. Will you never learn? Just because you put on a dicky bow and you stand around like a gangster out of a B movie doesn't mean you've gone up in the world. It's still clubs. It's still dodgy deals in back rooms with fellas tanked up to the eyeballs."

Some things Jackie never understood. Barry was going to pay him a decent wage, plus overtime. Whatever else he might be involved in, this bit of business was on the level. It meant Jimmy could start his dreams up again, make it up to Jackie, be someone.

"I want my own proper shop," he told Jackie. "This way, I'm going to make big money with no overheads. Couple of years, and I'll get that shop. Centre of town. Prime site. Honest. Trust me. In a couple of years we're going to have that business. Our business."

Jackie smiled indulgently. "Oh, Jimmy. What are we going to do with you?"

"What I'm doing, I'm doing for you. You know that, don't you?"

She deserved so much after what he'd put her through. On the coach to Birmingham, Jimmy passed the time mentally decorating a house for the two of them. Three bedrooms, no, four. And an en suite bathroom.

Birmingham was confusingly brilliant. The first surprise was Joe Halsall. For a start, she was a woman. A sharp eyed, smart piece from the Smoke. Jimmy wasn't sure if he fancied her or not. All the bits were in the right places – good figure, straight features, shiny brown hair cut into a businesslike bob, but the knowing, hard expression put him off. She was bright enough and welcoming to Jimmy. Anyway, Barry was probably giving her one.

"Welcome to Halsall Leisure," she said. Her handshake was as firm as a man's. "We'll get you started right away."

Jimmy took to the job like a Kray to crime. They even paid for him to take driving lessons.

"Can't have you driving around illegally," Barry had said. "I don't want anything messing up my club."

Which was fine by Jimmy. At the end of the month, he took and passed the test. No-one made a big deal out of it. Why should they? They didn't realise it was his very first official qualification.

The only problem was getting in contact with Jackie. He meant to, but somehow the days slipped by and he hadn't quite got as far as a phone. It was impossible at night, of course, and she'd be working during the day. He called once on a Saturday afternoon, but she was out. When he tried the next day, it was engaged.

Oh well, he thought. He'd sort it when he got back. She'd be so pleased to see him doing well, she'd forgive him. The fortnight turned into a month. Halsall Leisure had outlets in Coventry and Jimmy was sent there to cover for a bloke who'd got beaten up by a customer.

"He was an idiot," said Joe. "Lost his cool and ended up in trouble. So you be careful, Jim. I can't afford to lose good staff."

Good staff, eh? The place in Coventry was noisy and packed, full of kids trying it on. Jimmy loved bossing them about. Especially turning away packs of lads.

"Ok, boys, on your way," he'd say, with one eye on the groups of girls waiting to come in.

He got back to Liverpool at the end of November and walked straight into trouble. For a start, Jackie wasn't remotely pleased to see him. He tried to apologise, but she wouldn't listen. Apart from anything else, he forgot her birthday. And nothing he said would convince her that the club was a legitimate enterprise. To pour salt into the wounds, every time he arranged to take her out, Barry needed him to run errands.

Jimmy knew it would take time to bring her round, but she'd forgive him eventually. More serious was the row between Rod and Di. With Jackie in such a mood, Jimmy naturally sought refuge with his nephew, only to find Di was staying with neighbours and Rod was nowhere to be found. He'd left the police and was now a security guard. Jimmy was stunned, so taken aback he even braved Julia Brogan to find out what was going on.

"There was an incident," she reported, full of self importance.

"What do you mean, an incident?"

"Diana was – erm . . ." Julia brought her mouth close to Jimmy's ear. He could smell her lipstick and lavender talc, but the only word he could make out was 'rape'. She drew back and continued the tale. ". . . only our Rod wouldn't believe her. He thinks she's just made it up."

"Hang on. Why would she want to make up something like that?"

"Because she knew the fella and went upstairs with him at a party. Our Rod thinks she panicked after and had to find an excuse."

Jimmy could feel his hackles rising. Diana was a favourite. She wouldn't make up a thing like that. "Who was he?"

"That's the worst thing. You know the deputy headmistress at Brookside Camp? His son."

"You what? That smarmy looking git who used to have a flick?" Jimmy remembered Peter Harrison alright. He'd been staying with his parents in Brookside Close. Two doors away from Rod and Di.

Di was taking him to court. Date rape, they called it. But rape was rape in Jimmy's book. The hearing was set for 11th January. There was a family conference at the Farnham's, where Diana was staying. Jimmy wasn't too thrilled with them going through all the proper legal channels. Especially when the defendant's parents were dead rich and could afford some smart arse barrister. It was all very well for posh Patricia Farnham to mouth off about legal remedies, but where did that leave the working classes? On the scrap heap, as usual.

"I should go over the road and sort that Peter Harrison out meself," Jimmy said, hardly able to contain his anger.

"You do, Jimmy Corkhill, and you and me are history," said Jackie, just as mad. She shook her finger in his face. "I'm telling you."

"I might have known," Julia put in her twopen'orth. "It's support the girl needs. Not the Corkhills rowing and throwing their fists about."

Everyone started drivelling on about whether Diana could go through with the court case. Jimmy's blood pressure was threatening to explode.

"The only way to sort this out is for me to punch a third nostril through that Peter Harrison's face."

He had to promise to keep away. It would upset Diana too much.

At least he had La Luz as a distraction. Opening night went well and they were turning people away on New Year's Eve. Best of all, Barry gave him a company car as a Christmas present. An Astra GTi. Jimmy was definitely on his way up.

Jimmy made sure he was free on the day of the court hearing. He met Tracy, Julia and Patricia Farnham in the waiting area. They took up one bench. Diana stood next to them with her father. The next bench was full of Harrisons: father, mother and rapist son. Jimmy could hardly keep his seat for frustration.

Diana gave her testimony bravely and clearly. It was obvious how upset she was. Jimmy wanted to put his arms round her, she looked so alone swamped by the witness box. When Peter Harrison's barrister started laying into her, Jimmy gripped the rail to stop himself mouthing off. The posh accent ringing confidently through the court room made his stomach churn. The bastard was enjoying himself. It was a performance. He put it to Mrs. Corkhill that she'd led the defendant on. He put it to her that she'd said yes, then changed her mind. He put it to her that she was frightened about what her husband would say. He put it to her and put it to her and put it to her.

Jimmy couldn't stay to hear any more. He stumbled back to the waiting room, keeping track of how long it went on by the growing pile of cigarette butts at his feet.

He was joined by the rest while they waited for the verdict. Jimmy couldn't stop himself making snide comments, louder and louder. He knew he was making things worse. Peter Harrison ignored him and Diana started to cry. Peter's father went over to the usher. Jimmy was immediately suspicious. What did he want? What trick was he trying to pull?

As they were called back in, Jimmy spotted Rod slip into the back of the public gallery. When the Not Guilty verdict was announced, he slipped out again. Tracy ran after him. The rest of the party waited for both of them to come back, but only Tracy reappeared.

"What did our Rod say, love?" Julia asked.

"Goodbye," Tracy replied. "I tried to get him to stay, but

he wouldn't hang around. As far as he's concerned, she's been found guilty."

Diana burst into tears, burying her head in her dad's chest and howling. Jimmy felt like crying himself. Another life ruined by Peter Harrison.

Tracy was also crying. "I tried to get him to stay," she sobbed. "But he wouldn't. He's gone."

The Harrisons were making their way down the stairs. Jimmy heard them talking about champagne and celebrations. They didn't care that Diana would never recover from her ordeal. They didn't care about justice. All that mattered to them was that they had the money to pay for some posh brief who could run rings round an ordinary girl like Diana. She never had a chance. What sort of a celebration would she have?

Mr. Harrison shook hands with their solicitor, thanking him for his help. Jimmy exploded with rage.

"That's right," he yelled, his words ringing up the stairwell. "Go on. All shake hands with your posh solicitor. So your nice little son's got into trouble, has he? Going to cost you a bomb, isn't it?"

"My son is innocent," Harrison hissed.

"Innocent? You don't know the meaning of the word. Everyone knows you can buy your way out of trouble if you've got a big fat wallet in this dump of a country. But that still doesn't make him innocent."

"No. The jury does that," Mrs. Harrison chimed in.

"But it's the judge who tells them how to think, isn't it? And we all know whose side he's on. If you're working class, you don't stand a chance."

The sound of truth echoing through the establishment

maddened Harrison into action. He leapt at Jimmy, only to be restrained by his wife and son. Jimmy was dragged away by Julia and Tracy and pummelled into a minicab.

They held a post mortem over a pizza in the salon. Jimmy was distracted, brooding on how he could get even with Peter Harrison. Diana was family. He owed it to her and to Rod to do something.

"You're very quiet, Jimmy," Julia commented. "Considering you were shouting out before."

"Actions speak louder than words," he replied.

"What are you talking about?"

"Peter Harrison. He might have got off in court, but this is the real world. I haven't passed my sentence yet. He's soon going to find out what justice is about."

Chapter 12

Jimmy ate, slept, drank and dreamt of revenge. It was twice as bad as Joey Godden. At least his brother's murderer had been banged up. Too working class to be able to take advantage, the weight of the law had come down on him. But Peter Harrison had walked free. Declared innocent. Such a nice lad. Educated. Office job. Someone like that couldn't possibly be a rapist.

He didn't even have the decency to get out. Every time Jimmy saw him sauntering down the Parade, it was all he could do not to attack him. Barry warned him not to start anything. La Luz didn't need that kind of trouble. The most Jimmy could do was hiss and spit, like a castrated tom cat. Cleaning up the vomit outside the club one Friday night, he managed to push his bucket of filthy water under Peter's feet. It tripped him up and made him look a fool, but it was nothing. Nothing.

The feeling of powerlessness drained him, took his energy. Peter Harrison was stealing his life. He sauntered past him once too often. Before he had time to think about what he was doing, Jimmy was following him home. There was a quiet pathway linking the Parade to Brookside Close. Peter grew uneasy as he walked further from human contact. His arms stiffened and his pace speeded up till he was almost sprinting.

Jimmy was pleased. Give him a taste of his own medicine. When Peter had gone through the front door, Jimmy crept round the back. There was no plan. All he wanted was to confront his family's enemy and make him suffer.

"What d'you think you're playing at?" A voice behind him made him jump. An arm clad in a distinctive red coat landed heavily on his shoulder. Barry Grant. "I warned you."

"I just want to smash his face in."

"I've already told you. I don't want any of your pathetic heroics rebounding back on me at the club," Barry said angrily. "You probably wouldn't stand a chance anyway. He's half your age."

Jimmy couldn't believe what he was hearing. This was supposed to be one of the hardest men in Liverpool. "You're going soft in your old age. D'you know that? A couple of years ago, you'd have been with me. Ready to kick his head in."

"A couple of years ago, Jimmy, I wouldn't have touched you with a barge pole. I want things done right here. So if you work for me, do as you're told. Don't do anything dodgy behind me back. Forget about Peter Harrison."

Jimmy answered with a shrug.

"If you don't listen to what I'm saying and stop giving me hassle, you're out." Barry put a heavy paternal hand on his shoulder. "It's up to you."

He had no choice. Not really. He had to keep the job if he was ever going to get on. It was a mystery why Barry had taken him on in the first place. They'd never exactly been friends and after the Kowboy Kutz fiasco, you'd think he'd have been glad to see the back of Jimmy. Better not to push it. Every time he so much as thought of revenge, he'd catch a glimpse of that elegant red trench coat.

After an enthusiastic opening, the club was going through a sticky patch. The novelty had worn off and La Luz was getting distinctly quiet. They needed something to attract the young, free and well heeled.

"Rave night," Barry said. "Wednesday."

"You're joking, aren't you?" Jimmy was appalled. "I've heard about them. The kids are all sky high on drugs. D'you know what you're letting yourself in for?"

"I'm handling this, alright? You concentrate on your job as head of security. Any trouble? It's down to you to sort it out."

The first one caused no end of trouble. Kids crashing out all over the place. Residents half a mile away called to complain. As for the bogs, they were the most disgusting Jimmy had ever seen. And he was the one who had to clean them up. Joe Halsall came down and was not impressed. Jimmy heard her and Barry arguing, so he was surprised and resentful when Barry told him there was to be another rave.

"After last time? Are you out of your mind?"

"This time, you'll search everyone." Barry had that determined, unarguable look on his face.

He had a bit of a laugh, frisking the girls. A couple put up a token protest, but it was hardly an intimate body search. The word must have got around, because Jimmy found very little. The evening was going well until someone called in the bizzies. At first, Jimmy thought it must have been some nosy neighbour, then he caught sight of Joe melting into the background.

A couple of days later, she took him to one side.

"I don't know if you've sussed it yet, but this club's got money problems," she said. "I'm talking big dough."

"I thought we were doing alright."

"No, we're not. And if Barry carries on the way he's going now, you'll be out of a job before you know it."

"You what?" Jimmy was horrified. "This place should be a little gold mine."

"It could be, if it weren't for Barry trying to make money running stupid raves for kids. We're not going to get rich on their pocket money, are we? And it's not good for business, him upsetting the police. I just thought you should know the form. He's got no future in this place."

Jimmy didn't quite trust her. She seemed plausible, but there was that business with the police. "I thought you and Barry were equal partners," he said cautiously.

"We're nearly bankrupt. He owns half of nothing."

What she wanted was to get Jimmy on her side. He wasn't sure. On the one hand, Barry had given him the job and he was family, more or less. On the other, it looked like it would be Joe paying his wages.

A few hours later, Barry was the one looking for support. Joe was demanding twenty-five grand from him to keep La Luz afloat.

"She's trying to screw me out of this club," he told Jimmy. "I'm going to need someone on my side. Someone I can trust. You know what I mean?"

Jimmy pledged allegiance for the second time in one day. It was like living in a pressure cooker in the club, with Joe and Barry taking turns to fan the flames. Joe attacked him with practicalities and facts. Takings were at a standstill. Barry was all washed up. Stick with her. Barry used a cold kind of emotional blackmail. Who got him out of trouble? Who got him the job? What about loyalty?

Jimmy's loyalty was to the side that paid him. The winning

side. The problem was deciding which that was. Barry was convinced that Joe was cooking the books. He tore the office apart looking for a second set of accounts. It gave Joe the excuse she'd been looking for and she ordered Jimmy to keep him out. Her partner was barred from the club.

Barry wasn't going to take that lying down. He was round as soon as the coast was clear. Jimmy blocked the door with his body, but he still listened to what Barry had to say.

"Remember who got you that job, Jimmy. How long d'you think you're going to last without me on the scene?"

Jimmy protested that he was on dodgy ground if Joe even spotted them together.

"Well, she won't see you with me," he countered. "I just want you to do something for us."

Jimmy opened the door a crack. " Like what?"

"I want you to let me into the club about half nine tonight. I'm gonna torch it. It's my building. I get the biggest payout on the insurance."

Of all the daft ideas. Jimmy wanted no part of it, but Barry ignored his protests. He said he'd be back in an hour and Jimmy was to let him in. Should he or shouldn't he? Was he on Barry's side or Joe's? Jimmy's allegiance swung from one side to the other like a pendulum as the hours ticked by.

"Jimmy," Barry hissed through the door. "Come on. Let me in."

Barry. Joe. Barry. Joe. BarryJoeBarryJoeBarryJoe. Barry.

Jimmy opened the door. Barry was carrying a petrol can. It was real. He was actually going to do it. At the back of the main room were some booths with upholstered seating. He started splashing petrol over the them methodically, creating regular stripes of wetness. The smell quickly went to Jimmy's head and stomach, making him sick and bewildered. What happened to all this talk about wanting a straight business? What about his job?

"This is crazy," he protested.

"That bitch deserves it," Barry replied. His anger was so cold it wouldn't melt in the blaze. His face, set and grim, looked almost unhinged.

Jimmy couldn't bring himself to leave Barry there. It was too dangerous. For once, he was in over his head. He might be good facing up to people, but what did he know about fire?

Barry told him to go.

"I'm not going anywhere," Jimmy said. "I'm not having you blowing yourself up on my conscience. I'm not leaving this place. You don't know what you're bloody doing."

Barry stopped dousing and straightened up. "I've done it before, haven't I?" A hint of a smile cracked the mask. "Remember your little squat shop? Kowboy Kutz."

"You what? You torched my shop?" It took a few moments for Barry's words to sink in. Then Jimmy roared. "You bloody did, didn't you?"

"I thought it was pretty obvious. I thought you'd've well worked it out by now."

It was Jimmy that exploded, not the bricks and mortar. "You ruined my whole future. That shop. I was getting my act together with that shop. Me and Jackie's future."

"It was my shop, Jimmy. It went up pretty smartish, though, didn't it?"

The ruthless bastard. Jimmy leapt on Barry, sending the petrol can spinning, it's contents spraying over the dance floor. His rage gave him the strength to floor the younger, fitter man. They rolled over and over in the petrol, Jimmy landing kicks and punches where he could.

"Hey, what's going on?"

Jimmy felt himself hauled off and turned to face Mick Johnson.

"I thought this place was being robbed. What's all this about?"

Barry stood up, wiped blood off his mouth. "I'll get you for this, Jimmy," he said. And walked quickly out of the club.

First thing next morning, Jimmy went to find Joe to tell her what had happened, including Barry's torching of Kowboy Kutz. He was in no doubt about whose side he was on now. She was shocked and angry, but in control.

"Leave it to me," she said.

"Listen. Faffing around's no good. He's dangerous and he said he's going to get me. He needs sorting. Properly."

Joe poured him a drink to calm his nerves. "Don't worry, Jimmy. I think I know a way. I'm sure that you and I can get rid of him."

"How? What are we going to do? I want him to suffer. I want him to suffer like me and Jackie did. I want revenge."

"Don't you worry, Jimmy. You'll get it."

When Jimmy reported for work that evening, he found Joe in a cheery mood. She asked him to sample some brandy, saying she had to make a decision about which brand to stock. It was a task to warm the cockles of Jimmy's heart. Just the thing he needed for his jangled nerves. Jimmy could sink enough pints to put three men under the table, but he wasn't so immune to spirits. Especially when the bottle was left under his nose. Before long, he was in a pleasant state of affable euphoria.

Joe laughed at him and told him to take the night off. She'd arranged for Barry to come in for a quiet word and didn't want any trouble. Besides, he was almost too drunk to stand. Jimmy fumbled for his car keys, but Joe took them from him. Better to walk home than risk an accident in his state. As he went out, he passed Barry in the foyer. Joe was waiting for him with a couple of heavies. Jimmy shut the door softly behind him. He hoped they'd finish off what he started the night before.

The pavement was far too narrow to walk down. The council ought to do something about it. Slabs broken. Lampposts in the way. Safer in the road. Jimmy meandered happily in the region of the white line.

About half way home, he became aware of a car behind him. Oops. Better get out of the road. As he teetered to the right, it veered with him. He staggered left, the car changed direction. Odd. Why didn't it just overtake? Like it was following him.

He turned round. Barry Grant. Jimmy recognised the Frontera and its driver. There was no mistaking the red of his overcoat, even though his face was hidden by the headlights' glare.

Jimmy stood in the middle of the road, hands on hips. "What d'you want, Grant?" he challenged.

The answer came in a roar of the car's engine as it lurched towards him. Jimmy tried to run, but there was no time to reach the pavement. He heard, rather than felt, the thump as he was mown down. Then came a searing pain in his chest and unconsciousness.

Chapter 13

Joe was one of the first to visit Jimmy in hospital. She wanted to know what had happened.

"It was a hit and run," Jimmy said bitterly, through the pain in his face and arm. "Only I saw who did it. Everybody's favourite property developer. Barry Grant."

Joe's expression hardened. "He's dangerous," she said. "The man is a psychopath. If Barry had got his way, you'd be measured for a coffin by now. Do the right thing and tell the police. I'm sure DI Kent would be very interested."

Jimmy wasn't convinced. He wanted revenge, but rat on someone? To the bizzies? That was going a bit too far. Also, he was still wary of Joe. That DI Kent had been hanging around the club a bit too much for his liking. He'd appeared when there'd been trouble earlier. Jimmy was pretty sure that Detective Inspectors aren't normally expected to take part in night club brawls.

On the other hand, Jackie wanted him to go to the authorities. She was dead worried and blamed it all on the club. Barry was well known as a bad lad. Just the kind to go for a dodgy set-up like La Luz.

"He tried to murder you, Jimmy," she said. "Go to the police. For my sake."

In the event, DI Kent was happy to come to him. He'd

been after Barry for years. Jimmy felt awkward giving a statement with only the ward screen for protection. He still wasn't one hundred per cent sure he was doing the right thing, but maybe justice would be done officially, for once.

The word was that Barry had gone to ground, so Jimmy was stunned to find him at his bedside one visiting hour. He actually had the nerve to claim it wasn't him driving the car.

"I bloody saw you," Jimmy said.

Barry shook his head. "You didn't see me." He emphasised the last word heavily.

"You were winding me up, I thought," continued Jimmy. "He's gonna stop, I thought. But you come straight at me."

"Jimmy, stop it, will you? You're paranoid. Look. I was sitting in the club with her when you got knocked down. You've gotta believe me. On me mother's life . . ."

"Mother? She wouldn't wanna know you. The coppers will have you and I'll face you in the dock, because you're going down for this one."

"Don't be stupid." Barry sounded desperate. "Joe Halsall's got you wrapped around her little finger."

Jimmy wasn't going to listen to any more of this crap. He hollered for the nurse and as quickly as he came, Barry was gone.

Barry was arrested and remanded in custody. Bail was refused. It was something of a relief to know that he wasn't going to be around when Jimmy left hospital. The injuries had looked bad, but they were mostly cuts and bruises. His broken arm was the worst thing. Two weeks later, he was ready for work.

Jackie pleaded with him not to go back.

"I hate bloody clubs," she wept. "I hate everything about them. Jimmy, your boss tried to kill you."

"Yeah, and he got caught, didn't he?" Jimmy was in a buoyant mood. With Barry banged up, he had nothing to fear. " He got caught and he's going down. And he's not my boss. Joe Halsall is."

"All I want you to do is to get another job. A safe job. Any other job except work in night clubs."

"I'm doing this for us. Barry Grant's already ruined my future. I am not having him ruining it again."

Joe was so pleased to see him, she cracked open the champagne. DI Kent appeared just as the cork popped. He brought glad tidings. Barry's application for bail had been turned down. Despite Barry getting hold of a top-notch lawyer.

They drank the afternoon away. DI Kent was knocking it back like no one's business. He left at six to go on duty. Jimmy was amused to see he wasn't even swaying. There was a hardened drinker if ever he saw one. Joe persuaded Jimmy to finish another bottle before he started work.

An apologetic cough made them turn away from the bar. A strange little man in a loud check jacket and a fishing hat stood grinning at them. He introduced himself as a friend of Barry's.

Jimmy was instantly suspicious. He didn't trust the nasal, London twang or the way he couldn't pronounce his R's. Joe was on edge too.

"Who are you, exactly?" she asked.

"Just a friend," he answered. "Did you know Barry let me show your books to my accountant?"

"He had no right to do that."

"Very interesting reading. Quite a lot of money gone astray, it seems."

"It's got nothing to do with you. What do you want?" Joe was getting rattled.

"I'm just worried about Barry. I think he might have been set up. What do they call it? Framed." He looked Joe straight in the eye. All at once his monotonous tone stopped sounding harmless.

Jimmy was unnerved. "He's trying to wriggle out of it. I know what he's like."

The bloke turned to him. "The thing is, he mightn't be the only one who's been set up. Barry said that he and Joe fell out over these discrepancies."

"Those books were available to him any time he wanted to check them," Joe said.

"I'm not so soft that I can't see there would be a very good reason for someone to want Barry out of the way."

"What is all this crap?" Jimmy jumped down from the bar stool. "Barry Grant tried to murder me."

"Did he? Are you sure?" Now it was Jimmy who got the full force of the bland blue eyes.

"I was there wasn't I?"

"But did you see *him*? You saw his car, but did you see his face? Did you see who was driving?"

Joe lost her cool. "Get this creep out of here. He's just doing Grant's dirty work for him," she yelled.

Jimmy was only too happy to oblige. The little creep had almost hypnotised him with his insinuations. He marched him through the club to the front door.

"Out," he said firmly. "And don't bother coming back. Alright?"

The man tucked a business card into Jimmy's top pocket.

"Take this," he said. "You may want to talk to me when you've thought all this through. You've been set up, lad, by her."

"Just do one, will you. Go on."

"She's been swindling Barry for months. Don't you think it's kind of funny that when he finds out he lands up in Walton Jail? I call that a bit of a coincidence. Did you really see Barry driving that car? Barry says you usually drive home. How come you walked that night?"

Jimmy was forced to stop and think for a moment. The answer made him uneasy. "Joe suggested it."

Oscar Dean. That was the name on the card. Jimmy had plenty of opportunity to mull over what he'd said as he served and swept and mopped. Could someone have set Barry up? It was unbelievable. But then, so was Barry trying to mow him down in the first place. The words kept ringing in his head. "But did you see his face?" Jimmy had to admit what he'd seen was the car and the coat. They were so much a part of Barry, but someone could have nicked them.

Jimmy took his worries to Joe. She was less than sympathetic when he reported what Oscar had said.

"He was talking out of his backside," was her opinion. "Anyway, it's got nothing to do with you."

"It's got a lot to do with me, if someone tries to run me down. What if someone has tried to set Barry up?"

"You saw him, for goodness sake," Joe said in exasperation.

"I can't be sure."

Joe came up close to Jimmy. All of a sudden she was steel and flint. "You saw him, Jimmy. You saw him and you made a statement to that effect to the coppers. If you want to keep this job, you stick to what you've said."

No way was Jimmy going to be bullied by a tart. The way she reacted, he knew something fishy was definitely going on.

As soon as he could, he went down the police station to withdraw his statement. DI Kent was furious, convinced that Barry had been getting to a material witness.

"You're not backing out on me, are you?" he said.

"I don't want to see an innocent bloke go down – even if I do hate his guts. Barry Grant is innocent. I know him. I know what he's like."

"Who the hell else do you think tried to finish you, if it wasn't Barry Grant?"

"I don't know, but I couldn't swear in court that it was definitely him." It sounded feeble, even to himself.

"You'd better. You made a statement and now you'll stick to it. I could do you for wasting police time. Let's see how that looks on your law sheet." Jimmy backed off – he didn't want to end up arrested himself. There had to be another way.

In desperation, Jimmy went round to Oscar's. The house was incredible. At least five bedrooms with en suite bathrooms. There were gold taps in the kitchen and the guest loo. White carpet two inches thick was laid throughout the ground floor. The garden must have been a good acre. Oscar was the genial host, but gave no clues as to how he'd come by his wealth. He welcomed Jimmy in, was anxious about his health and generally behaved like a benevolent old uncle.

However, he proved incredibly effective. His explanation of what had happened was simple and plausible. While Joe kept Barry occupied, one of her heavies lifted his coat and car keys and went after Jimmy.

When the penny finally dropped, Jimmy was ready to go round and sort Joe out his own way. "I'll do that bloody club," he shouted. "I'll do it now. She tried to have me murdered."

Oscar just smiled his calm and irritating smile. "You're a bit like Barry, aren't you? All knee-jerk reactions." He tapped his forehead. "Not thinking it out up here first. Look, if you really want to get things sorted out, the first step is to get Barry out of jail.

Suddenly it was easy. All Jimmy had to do was call in sick, then go back to the police. Flanked by Oscar's brief, he'd have no trouble withdrawing his statement.

In fact, it proved quite a laugh. DI Kent's face was a picture when Jimmy walked in beside this posh bloke in a suit. Two minutes later and the case against Barry Grant fell to pieces.

When Jimmy went back to the club that night, some miracle seemed to have happened. Joe was gone. It was as though she'd never existed. Instead, Barry Grant was in place behind the desk. He was about as pleased to see Jimmy as Jimmy was to see him.

"What's Grant doing here?" he asked Oscar.

"Oh, he works here," Oscar replied. "In fact, he's my partner, so he's your boss."

Oscar left the room to have a word with his solicitor. There was a pause.

"I'm not working for you," Jimmy said.

"Good. That settles it," said Barry. "You can come and collect your cards tonight."

"I haven't said I'm not working. I said I'm not working for you. I work for Mr Dean."

In no time, they were having a slanging match. It got so loud, Oscar was brought back upstairs.

"Raised voices," he tutted. "We don't like raised voices. Barry, my solicitor wants to see some of the figures. Give them to him."

Barry departed with an armful of buff files. It was as though

Oscar was directing the action and had deliberately got Jimmy on his own.

"Now, Jimmy, that really wasn't very intelligent, was it?" he said paternally. "You've got to learn to use your brain."

"But it's him. He wants to sack me."

"Of course he doesn't," Oscar continued in the same soothing tone. "He's just feeling a bit bruised, that's all. I'm relying on the pair of you to work properly together as a team. Harmony, James. That's how we like it. I'm particularly relying on you because you know clubs from the bottom up. Show me a man who knows a business from the bottom up and I'll show you a potential director. Another thing, Jimmy. I'd like you to keep a little eye on Barry."

Jimmy's spirits rose. Relying on him, eh? Keep an eye on Barry? He could do that. He'd be glad to. Barry came back in.

"Barry, I was just telling Jimmy I want you two boys to work properly together." Oscar put an arm around each boy's shoulders. "Team work, you know. No silly tempers. No threats of sackings. Team. Work. That's how we like it."

He pottered off to have a word about VAT returns. Barry and Jimmy could only look at each other in amazement. Who the hell is Oscar Dean?

Chapter 14

"Cheap and cheerful. That's what we want, lads," Oscar said cheerfully, showing off his abundance of teeth. Jimmy had to admit he seemed to have an instinct about the club scene. Where from was anybody's guess. Barry found out that his roots were in the building trade, but the rest was very vague. In the end, they shrugged their shoulders, were grateful for his support and got on with it.

He was generous with the money and supportive of Barry's plans for special nights. Raves definitely appealed. Lots of people in. Good publicity and you could charge a bomb for glasses of water. One idea of his own was a special telephone booth, with a direct link to a local minicab firm. It provided an extra service and a backhander from the taxis.

No sooner had Barry set a date for the relaunch rave, than Oscar disappeared off to Spain. He wasn't interested in the day-to-day running of the club, much to Barry's annoyance. Jimmy didn't mind. It gave him a chance to take a bit more on, show he could behave responsibly. He didn't want to always be the underdog, fighting to survive. He wanted to move on and move up.

Every half an hour, Jimmy did the rounds of the dark corners and toilets. A couple of lads caught his attention. They seemed to be making connections with different groups, having a quiet word here and there. Jimmy's suspicions were definitely roused when they sauntered to the bog with a shifty, casual air. He followed them in.

Jimmy watched as one of them pulled a small packet from his pocket. He collared them as they were about to go into a cubicle together.

"Alright, lads. What's all this?"

He grabbed the packet. It was a small plastic bag with a few red-and-yellow capsules. Jimmy felt his heart beat increase. Drugs. He actually had drugs in his hand. It took every ounce of concentration to remain cool.

"You two, out," he said firmly. With a fair amount of discretion, he saw them off the premises. They didn't seem too worried. Just laughed and put two fingers up at him. Jimmy watched them go. They drove off in a BMW. At their age. Neither lad could have been more than eighteen. Jimmy found himself hating them. Despite their youth they had money, and money gives you power.

The next night was far less hassle. A treat for the mortgage and Montego brigade. Sixties night. It was dead popular. The club was crowded out with the middle aged recapturing their youth and hiding their paunches under kaftans.

The punters were so respectable, Jimmy even had time to circulate. He noticed Brian Kennedy, Tracy's boss, drinking alone. They agreed that tonight was not the real thing.

"The place isn't choking with dope smoke, for one thing," Brian commented.

"Yeah, it's the teenagers who're getting back into all these hippy bands, isn't it?" Jimmy replied. "It's the kids at the raves I have to keep my eye on these days."

He told Brian about the incident the previous Saturday and

showed him the packet of capsules he'd confiscated. He didn't know why, but he'd kept them.

"What are they?" Brian asked. "Granny's little liver pills?"

"They're E, mate. Ecstasy, I'm telling you." Jimmy was still excited by his discovery. The pills seemed to move on the bar. He looked at them, fascinated by the unknown.

"Have you ever tried one?" Brian broke through his reverie.

"Me? Get out of it."

"Why not?"

"Because they're drugs, aren't they?" Even Jimmy wasn't that stupid.

"You're not chicken, are you?"

"Me? chicken?"

"Yeah. In case you turn into some drug crazed monster." Brian had a camp, teasing manner that Jimmy associated with all male hairdressers.

And he was not having any slurs on his macho reputation. "On one of these piddling little things?" he boasted. "Get out of it. I'm not scared, I'm just not into drugs. I'm an alehouse man, me. I've done over twenty pints in a session." He drained his glass by way of proof.

Brian looked at him with amusement. "Alcohol's a drug, isn't it? And nobody stops you drinking."

"Listen, I control what I drink," Jimmy said. "Drink doesn't run my life. Not like the way all these druggies end up."

Brian took a deliberate swallow of his mineral water. "I reckon if they legalised drugs tomorrow, they'd solve half the problem," he said slowly. "People just overreact, don't they? They're scared of something they don't understand."

He was at it again. Calling Jimmy Corkhill a coward.

"Hang on. Hang on. You're accusing the wrong fella, here,

mate." Jimmy was getting belligerent. "I'm not scared of nothing. Alright?"

Brian pushed the capsules towards him. "Go on. Try one, then."

"What? Here? Now?" Jimmy felt as if he'd been outmanoeuvred somehow.

"Why not? You can't be sounding off about something you haven't experienced."

Jimmy kept staring at the innocent looking red-and-yellow pills. They could have been indigestion tablets. He was wary and tempted.

"What makes you the big authority on all this drugs lark?" he asked.

"I've been around. I do a little."

It was believable. There was something glamorous about Brian. He obviously wasn't short of a bob or two, with one salon on Brookside Parade and another in Chester. Jimmy was impressed by the way he talked. Real gift of the gab, he had. His argument made sense as well. What harm could there be in trying E just once?

He swallowed a capsule with some beer and waited for his head to explode. Nothing happened. He put the rest in his pocket. After a quarter of an hour, a disappointed Jimmy went to inspect the toilets. While he was there, it all suddenly became clear, as though someone had switched a light on. He was happy. More than happy. Lifted right out of himself. As though he'd dropped years and pounds. He had so much energy he had to take it out on the dance floor.

If only the music had been faster, louder, stronger. Jimmy could outdance the lot of them. He twirled one middle aged matron after another round the floor. When they were all exhausted, he danced by himself.

Brian was looking on and laughing. Jimmy went over to him, taking the packet out of his pocket.

"I'm going to have another one of these. In fact, I might have two. I'm OK, because I'm telling you – the one I swallowed had no effect. I don't know what all the fuss is about."

Barry came up behind him. He didn't look pleased, poor sod.

"What are you doing?" he asked. Then he saw what Jimmy was holding. "Right. That's it, dickhead. You're sacked."

Jimmy knew he ought to mind, but he just danced out of the club. Back home, Jackie was in bed, dozing. God, she was gorgeous. She turned him on even in a brushed cotton nightie. He hadn't wanted her so much for years.

"Gerraway, Jimmy." She pushed him off. "What time is it?"

"Two o'clock in the morning," he replied, putting his arms round her. "And all's well. All's very well. In fact, I don't know when it's been better."

He snuggled into her hair, kissing and stroking her. By now, she was thoroughly awake.

"What's got into you?" she asked.

"It's a question of what's going to get into you."

It was the best session they'd had in years. Even when he'd given his all, Jimmy was still raring to go. He couldn't stay in bed. Jackie wanted to go to sleep and wasn't interested in seeing if she could do the twist after twenty years. In the end, he went downstairs and boogied to the record player, turned down low.

Reality hit the next day. Jimmy was exhausted. He felt like he'd been in a marathon followed by a fight. The first thing he had to do was square things with Barry.

No chance. Barry was adamant. Jimmy pleaded that it was only one tab and he'd flushed the rest away.

"You didn't flush your brains down the bog as well, did you?" Barry said.

"Look, I made a mistake, OK?"

"A big mistake. I told you – I don't want any drugs in this club."

End of discussion.

Jimmy went back that evening to hand in his identity card and to beg for his job again. To his surprise, Oscar was in the office with Barry. That man kept popping up like a jack-in-the-box.

When Oscar heard what had happened, he was sympathetic.

"Why did you do it?" he wanted to know.

"To see the effect," Jimmy replied, sheepishly.

Barry was not interested in any more talk. "We've got things to do here," he said. "So if you'd like to call back Monday, you can get the rest of your wages. Sorry."

"Hang on a mo, Barry," Oscar said. "Don't you think you ought to consult your partner before it comes to hiring and firing the head of security?"

"You said you wanted to keep the club clean. We don't want any weirdos around, do we?" Barry sounded exasperated. He'd been longing for an excuse to get rid of Jimmy.

"Oh I appreciate that. I think Jimmy does too," Oscar said. He turned to Jimmy. "How does it sound if we let you keep the job?"

"Brilliant." What more could he say? That was one in the eye for old Grantie.

"I think I'll have to override Barry on this occasion," Oscar continued. "We're all allowed one mistake."

While Jimmy was sorting out the drinks later on, Oscar took him aside for a quiet word.

"This place is in capable hands. You and Barry have different sorts of talents. You seem to be able to manage between you."

That was one thing Jimmy had noticed about Oscar. He was appreciative.

"Thanks, boss," he said. "Sorry about last night. I know I was out of order getting off me head when I should have been working, like."

"You know you made a mistake. That's good enough for me. I wouldn't mind a word to the wise, though."

"Go on."

"These lads who bring in the happy, happy pills – we'll just leave them to do what they do for a while, shall we?"

You could have knocked Jimmy down with a feather. "You don't want me to chuck them out?"

"We're not the police, are we? If they're stupid enough to do it, it's not up to us to stop them. They're not doing us any harm, are they? Bringing all this custom in. We'll turn a blind eye. If they didn't do it here they'd only go somewhere else."

It was a whole new world to Jimmy. His gut reaction had always been that drugs were a mug's game. Before he'd finished reeling from Oscar's comments, Brian pushed him into a new spin. He'd come over to see how Jimmy's head was and to continue their conversation from the night before. His argument was that just about everything's a drug – booze, fags, even coffee and tea.

"You wouldn't go around injecting yourself with tea, would you?" Jimmy pointed out.

"That's not what I'm saying, is it?" said Brian. "I wouldn't put a needle anywhere near me, I can tell you that."

"I bet you'd pop a pill or two though, wouldn't you?"

Brian didn't deny it. He'd been into speed at college. Jimmy wasn't surprised. That was typical of students. Especially the arty farty types. What astounded him was when Brian told him that he'd been offered something in La Luz only last week.

"Apparently, this club is fast becoming the place to go if you've got money to spend," he said in a low, confidential voice.

Jimmy could hardly believe it. He and Barry had been so careful. How had it slipped in? It seemed you could get whatever you wanted in that very room. Jimmy wondered how Brian knew.

"Look, I've got these mates, right," Brian explained. "What they do is this. They go out, buy a bit of gear, let it get into their system and then have a cracking night out. What harm are they doing to anybody?" He grinned. "If there are guys dealing in here, you're the one who's losing out. You could be helping people. You know, get what they're looking for."

Things were going a bit too fast for Jimmy. "Hang on. Are you talking about me helping you get whatever it is you're looking for."

"Not me personally. But I do know people who'd be interested. You could make a lot of money here, Jimmy. And I mean a lot."

It was all food for thought.

Chapter 15

A couple of days later, Brian was back. With a bribe. He held out a couple of twenties and hinted that he was very keen to find out what was on offer. Would Jimmy keep an eye open? What Brian really wanted was a price list.

"I'm not interested in anybody's drug deals," Jimmy hissed. "I just do as I'm told."

"You'd be doing a friend of mine a big favour." Brian tucked the money into Jimmy's top pocket. "Keep the cash anyway. Just in case."

Without meaning to, Jimmy found himself drawn into a whole new world. On the one hand, he knew druggies were the lowest of the low, losers spending their time begging and stealing before drowning in their own vomit or dying of overdoses. On the other, Brian was smart, rich and smooth. One of the upwardly mobile. He didn't fit the picture.

Now that Jimmy knew where to look, he was forever catching sight of young scallies with no qualifications, no work, nothing, yet they had flash cars and money to burn. They reminded him of his age. The more he watched what was going on, the more fed up and out of it he felt.

The connections were via the taxi drivers. Jimmy soon spotted the ones that were bent. The handovers were very casual. One of the kids would seem to be having a chat with a cabbie, one arm resting casually on the car roof. Then the hand would come down, a discrete flash of notes you could only see if you were watching for it and the buyer would hurry away to a dark corner.

So Jimmy had found out who to ask. Now it was a question of what Brian wanted.

"Charlie," he replied.

"You what?" Jimmy had never heard to term before.

"Cocaine," Brian explained.

This was way out of Jimmy's league. He could cope with happy, happy pills for soft teenagers, but not stuff you smoked and injected and got addicted to. From what he'd heard, you were down the pan if you so much as looked at it.

"Just leave me out, alright?" he said, backing off.

It was as if Brian could read his mind. "Look, Jim, I haven't got any druggie mates. We're talking solicitors, accountants, one guy is a doctor. They're just professional people looking for a better buzz. They're not smack heads. There's not a dirty syringe to be seen."

And there before him was the smartest bloke on the Parade. The most respectable, on a par with the Farnhams and far better dressed.

"Is that true?" he asked.

"Yeah. People who are willing to pay for a service if you can provide it."

Jimmy was always open to argument. Especially if he might profit by changing his mind. He was still wary, though.

"I don't like drugs. I never have."

"You did one more E than I did last week," Brian pointed out. He gave him £120.

Jimmy still wasn't sure.

"If you don't do it, someone else will."

The gear cost £80, leaving a net profit of £40. It was the easiest money Jimmy had ever made. No one batted an eyelid at La Luz's Head of Security getting friendly with the taxi rank. All part of the job. The second deal netted him even more.

He saved most of his new income and spent the rest on the house. Jackie was delighted with her new drinks cabinet and carpet. Telling her it was down to overtime was almost true.

It was Barry's turn to disappear to Spain, and Jimmy was left in charge. Why not? Didn't he know the business? Hadn't Oscar said he relied on him? What he needed now was something to prove his worth.

Another rave night, well run and profitable, was the answer. Only with both Oscar and Barry away, he'd need help. It took a bit of doing, but eventually Jackie agreed to help.

By now, Jimmy was on to all the tricks. Before the rave started, he turned off the water in the toilets. It was the only way to make a profit. Kids nowadays wouldn't buy proper drinks. Alcohol and ecstasy didn't mix. You had to charge them for good old H_2O and stop them getting freebies out of the bogs. Needless to say, Jackie didn't approve. If you only knew the half of it, Jimmy thought.

About half way through the evening, she found out. A couple of girls called her to come and help one of their friends who'd collapsed in the Ladies. She was gone ages, so Jimmy went to investigate. He found her bending over a kid who couldn't have been more than fourteen.

The girl was dead to the world. Jackie demanded that he call an ambulance. He refused point blank. By now, Jimmy

knew the form. It was obvious she'd had one E too many.
That was the last thing the club needed. Talk about bad publicity.

"I don't care if you do lose your licence," Jackie yelled. "I'm
not having a girl die on me."

"Jackie. Listen. It's not alcohol. She's taken a couple of E's.
Probably been sold a dodgy one." The trouble with ecstacy
was that it wasn't reliable.

Jackie was taken aback. "You mean drugs? How did she get
hold of them?"

"It goes with the territory. It's a club. It's a rave night.
What d'you think they were on?" Jimmy didn't want to explain, but he had no choice.

As he guessed, his excuses cut no ice with Jackie. She stood
up to find a phone. Jimmy grabbed her.

"Look. Call an ambulance and the police'll get involved.
Don't worry. It's happened before. Stay here and I'll go and
get one of the cabbies to take her to the hospital."

"Oh I see. It's a regular occurrence this, is it? You know
more about these drugs than you do how to stop it." Typical of
Jackie to blow things out of all proportion.

"It's club policy, right? As long as it's under control, Oscar
likes us to turn a blind eye. I manage the place and I know
what brings in the profits. Get real, Jackie. If they don't do it
here, they'll do it somewhere else, OK? So we might as well
make what we can out of it."

He left her watching the girl didn't choke on her own vomit
and went to get a cab. The crisis was averted and he heard
later that the girl recovered. Jackie was not impressed when
he told her. As far as she was concerned, drugs were drugs.
They were dangerous, evil and not to be touched. Brian's

arguments about alcohol and caffeine went straight over her head.

The best thing was for him to keep quiet. She'd come round when he had enough money for a deposit on their dream house. Already Jimmy had £500 put by.

Brian kept tempting him to try it, but Jimmy wasn't that stupid. He wasn't about to become an addict.

"I'm not addicted to it, Jimmy," Brian explained patiently. "I just snort a little coke like you drink a couple of pints of beer."

"Yeah, well you know where you are with alcohol, don't you?"

"You know where you are with coke. As long as you don't abuse it."

Jimmy supped his beer and made no comment.

"You still can't get your head round it, can you?" said Brian. "Look, I'll tell you what I'll do. I'll introduce you to some friends of mine."

"Coke heads you mean?"

"You call them coke heads, I call them friends. Professional people. Like Rod, he's a doctor. And his wife, Alex, she's reading for the bar. You look after them, Jimmy, and you'll start getting a whole new 30-something clientele in this club. The sort of people who spend money. That'll go down very well with your Mr Big."

He was right there. A bunch of middle class yuppies would be right up Oscar's street. Brian brought a group in a few nights later. Jimmy watched them while he was working. With their sharp suits and shoulder pads, they showed up the usual riff raff. Money and drink flowed. There was no arguing over whose round it was. Snatches of conversation drifted

Jimmy's way. He heard about houses and holidays, cars and children's shoes. No moans or whinges, just the sweet contentment of success.

They were still there at closing time and invited Jimmy to join them. Champagne was ordered. He was delighted. Pity everyone else couldn't see him going up in the world. However, the conversation was way over his head. Did he ski? No? Oh well. Then they started talking about some posh film director Jimmy had never heard of. Every time he opened his mouth he made a fool of himself. But they wanted him there. They offered him champagne like he was one of them.

Every so often, one of the group would exit discretely towards the toilets. Brian told him sotto voce that they were snorting, not shooting up. Why didn't he try some?

Thoroughly intimidated, Jimmy refused. "I'll stick to the bubbly," he said.

When it came to the middle classes, Jimmy went from one extreme to the other. He'd love to have the clout and confidence that went with money. In his day-dreams, he imagined himself discussing holidays in the Algarve and foreign cinema with the best of them. Yet he bitterly resented the sheer luck that meant they were on top and he was left floundering in the bottom of the barrel.

Maybe Brian was holding out the hand he needed to help him up. He asked him to provide some gear for a party he was holding and gave him an invitation. Jimmy was flattered, but Jackie wasn't too keen. She had no time for Brian, thought him too smooth, but agreed to go for her husband's sake.

It wasn't quite what he'd expected. Brian couldn't remember Jackie's name and seemed almost surprised she'd come. Jimmy was detailed to take coats and hand round the drinks. Well, he was a mate. Mates help out, don't they?

Jackie took her glass and went to stand on the edge of the group of Brookside neighbours. Jimmy wasn't happy to see that Peter Harrison was part of it. He was sounding off about Oxford bloody University.

"Went to Oxford, didn't you?" Jimmy needled. "The place is full of murder and rapists. Then there's the Cambridge rapist. D'you reckon it's got anything to do with being too clever for your own good?"

He knew he was making everyone feel awkward, especially Jackie, who was crimson with embarrassment, but he couldn't resist it. Every time he saw the bastard, his hands curled with the itch to punch his head in. He couldn't watch him smirking with the in-crowd without trying to do something to make them see what he was. Trouble was, he was the one who ended up looking like a prat. They stuck together, that lot.

Jackie walked out, sick of watching Jimmy skivvying. At least it saved him the bother of making excuses for the main event of the evening. Peter Harrison was the last of the outer group to leave. Trust him to outstay his welcome. It was a great moment for Jimmy when he shut the door on him, knowing that he was well in. The only other people left were the ones who'd come with Brian to La Luz.

"Let the party commence," said Brian.

"Yeah." Jimmy was looking forward to it.

Brian held out his hand. "Cheers – and Jim. Thanks for helping out tonight."

"My pleasure. No problem."

"You won't have any trouble getting a cab on the main road."

It took a moment for it to sink in. He was being told to go. Jackie was right. Brian hadn't wanted him as a guest at all, just a lackey. An unpaid one, at that.

Jimmy took his fury out into the rain. A familiar figure was trying to hail a taxi. Peter Harrison. Jimmy went after him, hardly aware of what he was yelling. All he knew was that there was a well of anger deep inside him, where what Peter Harrison had done to Diana and what Brian had done to him were mixed in with all the little insults and put downs he'd suffered over the years.

There was no mistaking the danger in his face. Peter Harrison took to his heels. Jimmy chased after him, determined to get him once and for all. A taxi pulled up. Peter jumped in, leaving Jimmy outside, beating out his rage on the window.

Chapter 16

The money Jimmy was making was a great comfort. It didn't all come from the deals, either. Now that he'd proved himself capable, Oscar and Barry quite often left him to it. The result was that he worked all the hours God sent and was paid overtime for it. What was more, he enjoyed it.

In only a couple of months, he'd saved a grand. Enough for a deposit on a house. He told Jackie of his plans, but her enthusiasm failed to match his. They ended up having a sparring match in the Trading Post, with Ron Dixon as referee.

"I left my brains at home the day I married you," was her first sally.

"What's wrong? We can start hunting in earnest now, can't we?" Jimmy countered.

Jackie turned to Ron. "Soft lad here wants to put us in hock for the rest of our naturals, when I have trouble getting the week's rent from him."

"Not lately you haven't. I've been keeping straight lately, haven't I?"

"How are you on nine hundred and ninety-nine years?"

Jimmy brought out the killer. His building society pass book. "A thousand pounds do you? Straight up. I've been doing loads of overtime for Barry and Oscar and putting me wages towards my little house fund. And this is all the thanks I get."

Women. There was no pleasing them.

Responsibility was taking its toll. Barry had agreed to organise an important wedding, arrange the catering and so on. It was for the Farnhams in Brookside Close. People with money. Worth getting in with.

Oscar was in Spain and at the last minute Barry went out to join him. He left a note saying everything would be alright in Jimmy's capable hands. Ta very much, thought Jimmy gloomily.

The big day followed straight on from the stag night. Jimmy had joined in with a vengeance. His hangover had a hangover. He was so tired, he could barely see the barrels of beer he had to unload, let alone lift them. Brian appeared, irritatingly perky. He offered Jimmy something to help him out. Speed.

"You survived that E, didn't you? Come on, trust your Uncle Brian. It won't make you a smack head. It'll give you a power boost. Think of it as a sort of a pick-me-up."

Jimmy put the packet of powder in his pocket. "I'll need that, won't I? If I'm going to stay awake till closing time."

He decided he'd only use it if he got desperate. By the time the reception was due to start, he knew he had to do something to survive. The speed seemed to be burning a hole in his pocket as he handed round the champagne. Ducking into a corner of the marquee, he slipped the powder into a glass and drained it. Easy as taking Beechams.

The effect was much better than E. Euphoria was all very well, but it didn't help you do your job. The speed did exactly what Brian promised. Jimmy was buzzing, but with controllable energy. He felt as if he'd had a good night's sleep, having given up fags and booze for a month.

The wedding went like clockwork. Jimmy was dressed up in his best bib and tucker, serving drinks, making sure the food was being eaten, smiling at the bridesmaids and laughing with the men. He felt like a huge ball was starting to roll and he was on top, perfectly balanced.

He might have known something would happen to knock him off again. Brian turned up to the tail end of the wedding and announced that their usual deal was off. Jimmy was devastated.

"What about me?" he said in dismay. "I've been saving up for that house for me and Jackie. I'm relying on that money."

Brian shrugged. Not his problem. He hinted that something big was about to happen, but wouldn't say what it was. The only message he had was that their usual agreement was finished.

No way was Jimmy going to let him get away with that. Why did everyone always assume he was only small fry? Good for a dodgy little deal on the side, but not in the market when there was real money to be made. He pestered Brian for more details.

When he got them, he almost changed his mind. A huge shipment of cocaine was due to arrive and Brian was in for thirty thousand pounds. You could almost buy a house outright for that. That was way, way out Jimmy's league. Then he noticed the smug, amused smile trying not to break out on Brian's face.

Persuading Brian to cut him in wasn't easy. He went on about it being big league and dangerous. If he said Jimmy had to keep his mouth shut once, he said it a hundred times. As if Jimmy would grass. In the end, Brian reluctantly agreed to cut him in for ten per cent.

"Three grand?" Jimmy was daunted.

"Take it or leave it. That's the offer. And I need the money by Friday."

Jimmy took it. Brian promised him that they'd make up to five times their investment. Somehow he had to raise the money. The first fifteen hundred was easy. He took it from his savings and the cash put aside for bills. Once the deal was done, he could easily replace it. The rest of the week, he went crawling to every person he'd ever done half a favour for.

He was still short a grand. Barry was back by now, but not in a good mood. There was no chance of a sub. The most he'd agree to was a few hours off.

Jimmy slipped off home. Jackie had gone to visit Lindsey, so the coast was clear. Under the bed was an old brown suitcase, full of documents and keepsakes. Jimmy got it out. He felt beneath the piles of wedding and christening photos for a large envelope. There was the rent book, their birth and marriage certificates and two life insurance policies. Whatever else happened, Jackie had always paid these.

Jimmy couldn't help kissing them as he slipped them into his jacket. He felt a bit guilty, but there was no harm really. He had more qualms about borrowing her charm bracelet. It was in a red velvet jewellery box hidden in the wardrobe. Jackie had been collecting the charms for years. Every birthday or Christmas, people would add to it. Jimmy had bought her a couple of bits when he'd been flush, a beer bottle and a galloping horse. By now, it was worth a fortune. Oh, well. They'd only be gone for a few days. Jackie would never know.

His guilty conscience made him plead with Brian for more time. If he only had another week, he could get money somewhere else, he was sure of it. But Brian was adamant. He took the two grand in cash and insisted on getting the other by Monday.

"This is top quality stuff," he said. "Pure cocaine. It's going to be the easiest money you've ever made. You and me are going to be rich."

It was a great consolation for having to hock Jackie's bracelet and the policies. All he had to do was hand over the money, let Brian do the business and walk away with fifteen thousand pounds. He could promise Jackie a house in Crocky Park with all the nobs.

"Promise nothing to nobody," Brian said furiously when Jimmy handed the money over. "Keep your mouth shut till this all blows over, right? This isn't the national lottery, you know. You do realise what you're getting involved in?"

"Only what you told us. About it being on a ship somewhere."

"Careless talk, Jim." Brian's voice was low and urgent. "D'you understand what I'm saying? The deal's getting closer. The stuff's coming into the docks this week. It's heavy stuff going down here, you know. We're not talking knock-off videos. We're talking class A drugs."

That wasn't Jimmy's concern. "I'm just after making a quick few bob, that's all," he said. "I don't want to get involved in the other side of it. That's not my style. I'll leave that to you and your mates."

"You're already involved. If anything goes wrong, then we all go down together. You do understand what's at stake, don't you? Ten years behind bars at least. Do you think you could cope with that? What is it they say? If you can't do the time, don't do the crime. So. I'm not trying to scare you off. I just want you to understand exactly what you're getting involved in."

Ten years. Jimmy was definitely beginning to have second thoughts. Even more so when Jackie tracked him down at La Luz.

"Where's me bracelet, Jim?"

Jimmy tried to play innocent. "What bracelet?"

"Me charm bracelet. What've you done with it?"

"I haven't touched it. I swear to you." Jimmy was sweating with the effort of making up an excuse on the spot.

"Don't lie to me," Jackie yelled. "You know it's worth a fortune. You know it's one of the only expensive things I own, so where is it?"

Stall for time. "When did you notice it was missing?"

"I was going to phone the police, then I realised. Then when I was looking for the rent book, I noticed the insurance policies have gone and all."

"Look, I'll come clean with you. I swear you'll get them back, it's just I needed the money. For an investment." Jimmy was desperate. Jackie wasn't going to be put off this time. She wanted blood. "I need it for a horse. I know it sounds dodgy, but it's a dead cert. Honest."

Jackie exploded. "I don't believe you," she screeched, slapping at his face and arms. Anywhere she could reach. "I don't believe you. I don't believe you. Stupid, stupid idiot." Each word emphasised by a blow.

Jimmy could only back off and cower. "I did it for you. I did it for us. So we could get our dream home. A brand new house for the pair of us. You'll get your bracelet back."

"There's no such thing as a dead cert where you're involved. Everything you touch turns to a disaster."

"It's guaranteed this, I swear."

Jackie wasn't listening. She headed for the door. "If I don't get my bracelet back, we're finished. We're finished for good," she said. "This time I really mean it."

She did too. The thought of losing her brought Jimmy out in a cold sweat. He collared Brian to try and find out if his money had gone for good. The deal was supposed to go through the next day.

"So have you actually handed the money over then?" Jimmy asked, trying to sound casual.

"Is there a problem?" Brian said suspiciously. "Because it's a bit late in the day to be messing around."

He hadn't answered the question. Jimmy tried again. "So have you handed the cash over then? Mine and yours?"

"Am I detecting some second thoughts on the horizon?"

"Not from me, no." He didn't want Brian to think he'd lost his nerve. "It's the missis you see. Well, it's her money and that."

"She's hen pecked you into chickening out?"

"No. She thinks I've stuck it on a horse," Jimmy explained. "I'm just not so sure it's a good idea now."

"I knew this would happen. Your bottle's gone, hasn't it? You're losing it, aren't you?"

That was the one thing guaranteed to make Jimmy sure of what he was doing. He wasn't going to be called a coward.

"I've got to turn up there with thirty grand," Brian continued. "Three of it's going to be yours whether you like it or not."

"Fine. Forget Jackie. This is what I want."

And he meant it.

Chapter 17

Brian came over to the club later that night, with a sample of the goods. They went up to the office for some privacy. Jimmy poured himself a brandy.

"You're going to buy your dream house, aren't you?" said Brian.

"You've no idea what it's like," Jimmy replied. "Up in your posh flat. I've never had a place of me own. Always rented. They're either crappy council houses or damp little flats. I've always wanted my own place." Jimmy picked up the slip of clear plastic. It took up a square inch in the palm of his hand. "Just look. Me whole life could change. All for a bag of powder. That is going to get me a house."

"You want to know why?"

"I know a lot of people will pay good money to shove gear like that up their noses."

Jimmy turned the bag over and over. It seemed so innocent. Like Johnson's baby powder.

Brian took the packet from him. "It's time you found out," he said.

It was fascinating to watch. He took out a mirror, some of the white powder, a credit card and a fiver. No wonder coke was known as a rich man's drug. You needed a decent credit rating even to take the stuff. Using the sharp edge of the card, he formed two neat lines of coke on the mirror. Then, he rolled the fiver into a tube, put one end to his nose, the other to one end of a line and inhaled.

So that was snorting. Jimmy couldn't get his head round it. Sniffing up what looked like caster sugar. It was both ridiculous and intriguing. What was it about the stuff that made people steal and lie for it? Why was it so powerful it had to be banned?

"If you knew what I'm feeling now," Brian smiled.

He'd kicked his Italian shoes off and had put his feet up on the sofa. You'd never guess he was on drugs. He was nothing like the druggies you see on the telly. His skin was clear, he was well dressed, he wasn't sweating or doing crazy things or talking nonsense. It obviously wasn't doing him any harm.

Brian passed the fiver. Jimmy's hand reached out for it. He put it to his right nostril, lowered his head to the mirror and breathed in. His nose tingled as the stuff went up, like an inside itch.

If speed was high, then coke was broad. Within a quarter of an hour of taking the stuff, Jimmy knew there was nothing to fear. It was like getting an award, a pat on the back; cheers, mate, and thanks for a job well done. Confidence. He could handle anything life threw at him. Jimmy put his feet up on the desk and enjoyed.

"Sweet as a nut," he said. He raised his glass, decided he didn't need alcohol and smashed it against the wall.

The next day, Jimmy was slowly tortured by suspense. He couldn't keep his mind on anything until he saw Brian's well-groomed head poke round the door. From the grin on his face, it was obvious the meeting had gone well.

Brian tapped his pocket and signalled for him to come over.

Jimmy almost rubbed his hands with glee. He was about to collect fifteen thousand pounds. Cash.

The Jiffy bag Brian handed over seemed far too small to hold all that money. Too right. Jimmy pulled out a polythene bag of the now-familiar white powder.

He stared at it in disbelief. "What's this?"

"What were you expecting?" Brian asked. "A bin bag full of the stuff? Now put it away."

"Where's me cash?"

"What cash?"

"You said I was going to treble me money." The old feeling of being betrayed crept up Jimmy's spine. "What do you expect me to do with this?"

"Whatever you like, mate. I know what I'm going to do with mine."

"Hang on. You said you had someone to sell the stuff on."

"I have."

"So why can't you sell my share and all?"

"Jimmy. I'm not your bloody wet nurse." Brian sounded exasperated.

Jimmy started to panic. "You're the only one I've ever flogged drugs to. I wouldn't know where to start." He clutched at Brian's arm. "Don't do this to me."

"All you do is cut the stuff up, adulterate it with sodium bicarb or whatever you like and sell it off in smaller wraps. You'll have plenty of takers."

It was easy enough for him. He was used to the game. "I'm not even a drugs dealer, let alone some sort of nuclear scientist," Jimmy said resentfully. He'd been stitched up. Brian had gone back on his word.

"That's crap." Brian wasn't having any of Jimmy's moaning. "Now, look. I'm going back to the salon to stash my share. You get yours hidden before it burns a hole in your pocket."

Jimmy had been dropped right in it. Three thousand pounds and all he'd got to show for it was a bag of drugs. He pleaded with Brian to give him some contacts. The answer was still no.

"You're on your own."

"All I'm asking for is a few names. You can give them my number if you want."

"Look, I don't want my name and your name mentioned to anyone. It's too risky."

In a panic, Jimmy stashed the hoard under the wardrobe. Jackie came in at that moment and very nearly caught him. He'd managed to avoid her for days. Now she was in a foul mood. Her nose was pinched white with anger and her mouth was a grim line of lipstick.

"I want me bracelet." She went straight on to the attack. "And those insurance policies."

"Don't worry. It's safe." Just converted into class A drugs.

"In some bookie's pocket, you mean."

"Give me a chance, will you?"

"No. I want me bracelet and that money back now."

"It's not that easy."

It was so unfair. If only she'd hang on for a couple of days, he'd have a chance to sort things out with Brian, sell the stuff and everything would be hunky dory. As it was, he was forced to admit that he hadn't actually put the money on a horse. Knowing Jackie, she'd have gone storming off down the bookies and then the sparks really would fly.

Jackie wasn't in a mood to be fobbed off. As far as she was concerned, he was up to something. She accused him of being up to his old tricks again. The irony of it was that what he'd got into was far worse than she could ever have imagined. When he couldn't hand over the money, she went mad.

"That's the end of it," she yelled. "The lying, the stealing. Never knowing when you're going to jail again. Go on. Get out. Just get out of my sight."

She pushed him out of the door. There was only one thing for it. He'd have to persuade Brian to take the stuff at cost. Never mind the profit. The important thing now was to get Jackie's property back.

As if things weren't bad enough, Brian told him there'd been a big coke bust in town. It meant that he wasn't shifting any gear. Not his own and definitely not Jimmy's.

"I've taken precautions and made sure my flat's clean. I suggest you do the same," he advised. "Keep your distance and get your stash put away."

Jimmy made up his mind to get rid of the stuff as soon as he'd finished work. About half way through the afternoon, there was a commotion on the Parade. Jimmy stuck his head round the door to see what was going on.

A van and an unmarked car had pulled up outside the salon. Two plain clothes officers went in. There was a brief pause, then they emerged with Brian between them. Handcuffed. A crowd gathered to enjoy a bit of scandal. Through their heads, Jimmy caught Brian's eye. His expression was completely blank. Did it mean that he'd keep quiet? Or that he was going to drag Jimmy with him?

"If anything goes wrong, then we all go down together." That's what he'd said. Along with ten years behind bars. At least. Drug smuggling. And Jimmy was in it up to his neck.

He couldn't hang around to see what would happen. Any

minute now, the bizzies would be breathing down his neck. There was no proof of any connection between him and Brian Kennedy, apart from the Jiffy bag in the bedroom.

Terrified, Jimmy jumped into his car and drove home. He was panicking so much, he could hardly see through the windscreen. His mind was racing with plans for a getaway. Spain. That was where the criminals went. Barry'd lend him his flat. A fight with Jackie. Need to get away for a few days. It was believable enough.

By the time he got home, everything was a blur. The only thing he was aware of was the shaking in his hands as he threw trousers, underwear, toothbrush into a holdall. The bag of cocaine went into the inside pocket of his jacket.

"What're you doing?" Jackie had sneaked up behind him.

"I'm going back to the club for me wages, then I'm off."

"Where?"

"Anywhere. I've got to hide out for a bit," he told her. "You don't know nothing. You haven't seen me and you don't know where I am."

The hurt look on her face killed him, but there was no time for explanations. Driving got harder and harder. Sweat flooded down his face, into his eyes. He took wrong turnings, almost had an accident at a T-junction.

A ciggie. That's what he needed. A cigarette would calm him down. He felt in the glove compartment. Shit. Run out. Now what? No time to find a shop. Got to do something. Got to calm down. Got to speed up. Got to get out of there.

The packet of coke slid along the dashboard as Jimmy swerved in an effort to keep the car under control. What he wouldn't give for that wonderful feeling of confidence. Why not? What had he got to lose? Keeping one hand on the wheel and one foot on the accelerator, Jimmy managed to pile some coke on to a bit of old card. He had to turn away to get the stuff up his nose.

The relief was instant, like a bracing, cold shower, but in front of him was a white Rolls Royce. A wedding car, heading straight for him. Jimmy suddenly realised he was on the wrong side of the road. He swerved, barely scraping the wing mirror. The roller veered the other way.

Straight into a brick wall.

It all happened so fast. Jimmy's head was spinning. He heard the crash, people screaming, gleaming white metal compacting into scrap.

Must stop. Accident. My fault.

No. Too dangerous. Drugs. Prison.

Ten years. Ten years. Ten years.

Jimmy's foot wouldn't come off the accelerator. In two minutes, the horrendous scene had retreated beyond his rear view mirror. Another two minutes found him back at La Luz.

Once the cocaine was safely stashed in the toilet, Jimmy could breathe a bit more easily. He looked like death. Red eyed and skin like pumice stone. Barry believed him when he said he was ill.

The club was laid out for a reception. Jimmy had forgotten all about it. He'd been invited, as well. Two of Barry's neighbours were getting hitched. Everyone was going to be there.

It couldn't be them. Jimmy closed his eyes and prayed. Not them in the roller. Please God. Don't let it happen.

He knew it was useless. The news came through. There had been an accident. The wedding car had crashed. As a special treat, the groom had been allowed to drive. An ambulance had taken him away, seriously injured. With him was a young lad who'd been travelling with them.

The bride escaped without a scratch. Barry arranged for Jimmy to take people to the hospital to be with her. In a dream, Jimmy found himself going back along the route, offering bland words of comfort, knowing full well it was all his fault.

The news, when they got there, was appalling. The bride groom was dead and the boy was in the operating theatre. It was Tony, Ron Dixon's son. If he lived to be a hundred, Jimmy would never forget the look of bewilderment on his face.

The word went round that a silver car had been seen just before the crash. On a quiet road, in the middle of a sunny day, some hit and run no-mark had forced the car off the road.

Some no-mark high on drugs. Jimmy realised it was his fault. His fault that a man was dead. His fault a bride was widowed fifteen minutes after she pronounced her vows. His fault that Ron and DD were in a state of shock. It would be his fault if their son died.

Chapter 18

The next month was a nightmare, only Jimmy couldn't ever sleep. How he managed the journey to Spain without killing himself, he never knew. Oscar was surprised to see him, but very sympathetic when he heard about the domestic problems.

"You just stay a while here," he said. "Soon have you back on your feet. A few days away from the little woman will clear the air."

As if it was that simple. Oscar's Spanish club was closed for the winter, so Jimmy spent his time overhauling the building. He had a room and all the booze he could drink. Perhaps it was because he was drinking wine rather than ale, but he couldn't get himself drunk. The stupor, the blessed feeling of not being himself, never came.

He was desperate to find out what was going on back home. Although Oscar phoned his wife every day, the only news he had was the progress of his extension.

"Have you talked to Barry lately?" Jimmy tried to sound casual.

"Oh, I don't think there's any need, do you?" Oscar replied. "It's all very quiet this time of year. I think we can leave things in his capable hands."

For ten days Oscar left him more or less to himself, then took him to one side for a little chat.

"I wonder, James, if it wouldn't be a good idea to get back to good old Blighty," he said.

"You what?"

"England. I wouldn't like Barry to think we'd deserted him. How about popping back? I'm sure the little fracas between you and your good lady will have blown over by now."

He had to go, dreading what he'd find when he reached Liverpool. There could be a warrant out for his arrest. Ron Dixon was probably after his blood. As for Jackie – he didn't know what to expect there. If he could only convince her that a business deal had gone wrong, so he'd nipped across to Spain to lie low, she'd forgive him. She always did.

He wasn't ready to face the music. Instead, he went to Basingstoke to seek sanctuary with Billy and Sheila. There was no problem telling them he'd had a row with Jackie. That was all too believable. Only they kept on at him to ring her up. Sort things out. Every day, he'd try. He'd pick up the phone, dial the number. Once or twice, he even got as far as her answering.

"I can't, Billy," he'd say, defeated. "I'm not ready."

"Come on, soft lad," said Billy. "You're making things worse. She might have changed the locks on you by now."

After a couple of weeks, the need to know what was going on became more urgent than the need to hide. He'd been away a month. Surely the heat would have died down by now.

He said goodbye to his brother and headed north. Should he go home? The house looked the same. There was Jackie leaving for work. He could go up to her. Make his excuses. Find out.

His feet wouldn't move. It was as though he'd been cemented into the pavement. What if she told him Tony

Dixon had died too? Suppose she called the police? He deserved to be locked up, but he couldn't face it.

The Dixons' front door revealed nothing. Jimmy hung around the alley for hours, hoping to catch a glimpse of Tony. No one came in or out. The Close was deserted. Perhaps they'd seen him coming and scarpered to avoid the stench of his guilt.

The hospital. Please God, let them say he'd been discharged weeks ago. Mild concussion. Back to normal by now. The Dixons had gone away on holiday to recuperate.

The porter at the reception desk directed him to Intensive Care. Tony was in a side ward with glass on three sides. Like he was in a show case. He looked so small in the bed. There were tubes running out of his nose and wires attached to his chest. A bank of machines hummed and flashed, but Tony didn't stir. It was like he'd been imprisoned, tied down by medical paraphernalia. The wall above the bed made a bizarre contrast. It was covered with cards. In the centre was a red poster with GET WELL SOON picked out in gold. To the right was a section devoted to Liverpool Football Club. Jimmy remembered seeing Tony kick a ball around the Close, dressed in the familiar red shirt. He'd been mad on the game, like any normal, healthy teenager. Always on at his dad to get him the latest kit.

Now look where he was. Look who'd put him there. Jimmy pressed his face against the glass, letting his forehead go cold. He wanted to shake Tony out of his sleep, force him to wake up. Sheer frustration at what he'd done overwhelmed him. One moment of weakness had done this. Killed a man and put a young boy into a coma.

His face dripped guilt. Snot, sweat and tears poured out of

him. His skin smarted from the salt. Murderer. He could almost hear the screams. The accusations. But they were in his head. The ward was silent and Jimmy crept away again.

How could he get back to Jackie? Just let himself into the house as if nothing had happened? Suppose she'd changed the locks? He didn't dare go and see.

It was a question of hitting the right moment. Jimmy booked himself into a grotty bed and breakfast to wait. Several times he almost fell in with Jackie as she walked to and from work. Several times his nerve failed.

He rehearsed what he'd say to her over and over again. It took his mind off Tony. About the only thing that did. The sordid cupboard he was staying in was soon thick with the stench of old ale and half-eaten burgers.

Two days ticked by. Twenty-ninth of November. Jackie's birthday. Maybe a special occasion would be right. Jimmy bought a bottle of perfume and went round to the Trading Post.

Jackie looked up as he came in. Her customer smile faded when she saw who it was.

"Do you know what I've been going through?" she greeted him. "I've been worried sick."

Not a good start. Jimmy tried to make his excuses. She wouldn't listen. Nor was she impressed by the package he offered her.

"I don't want birthday presents from you," she snarled. "I wanna know where you've been."

He gave her the line about lying low and the business deal going wrong.

"I don't wanna talk about it, Jackie. I just wanna try and get on with things," he said.

"So you expect to walk back into my life as though nothing's happened?"

Jimmy realised that was exactly what he had hoped for. "I just want us to get back to normal."

"Do you?" Her voice became hard and loud. "Well, you're not on."

Ron came in from the stock room. He was on his way to the hospital. Jackie nudged Jimmy into asking after Tony.

"If I had one wish, it'd be to have him home and well for Christmas," said Ron. "So that's what I'm working on."

Jimmy was almost out of money. He couldn't afford the b. and b., so he decided to phone Oscar. After a few bites of humble pie, he got permission not only to start work again, but also to kip on the office couch for a few days.

Needless to say, Barry was not pleased when he heard. "If it was still down to me, your feet wouldn't flaming touch," he said.

As soon as he got a minute alone, Jimmy checked for the bag of coke under the bookcase. Miraculously, it was still there. He opened it. Looking at three thousand pounds worth of white powder, Jimmy felt his spirits lift for the first time in weeks. At least he still had resources.

To take his mind off Tony Dixon, Jimmy started a campaign to win Jackie back. Every chance he got, he waylaid her to apologise. Although she tried not to show it, he could tell she was softening. The days of filling the Trading Post with flowers were over, but at least he managed to remember their anniversary at the beginning of December.

"Birthday present and anniversary present," she said. "Fancy you remembering. It has made a change. Remember when you used to get a charm for me bracelet."

"How many times do I have to tell you I'm sorry," Jimmy said, exasperated.

"The one anniversary present that'd make me happy is getting me bracelet back."

He started to explain for the hundredth time.

"Oh no more stories, Jimmy. I know it's gone forever."

What she had in mind to earn her forgiveness was an ordeal by fire. Not that she knew it. As far as she was concerned, visiting Tony Dixon was simply the right and civilised thing to do.

"Don't be so soft," she said when he tried to get out of it. "You've known them since they moved here. We should show our faces." Then she delivered the ultimatum. "If you want to get anywhere near coming back home, you do this for me."

Ron was there when they arrived, with Mike, his eldest. Jimmy was stopped at the door by the look of hopelessness on their faces. The doctors had told them it was very unlikely Tony would ever come round.

The news hit Jimmy like a demolition ball in the chest. He could hardly keep from sobbing in front of everyone. The thought that he could have killed the lad, destroyed not only his own future but Ron's as well, was unbearable. The ironic thing was that he could feel a warm wave of fellow feeling from the others. It comforted them to know that he was grieving too.

Ron was still talking. "That's what the doctors are saying. It's not what I'm saying. There's places and that in America. I'm sure of it. They may be able to help. I'm not going to give up."

Jimmy grabbed the straw. "You mustn't give up, Ron. There must be someone, somewhere, who can cure him. We've gotta find out."

"We'll be looking. And while we are, we'll be fund raising."

Suddenly Jimmy knew what to do. " I'll be fund raising. I don't.care how long it takes, I'll get you the money, Ron. And I mean legally."

It was the only way to put right what he'd done. There was always a cure if you could afford it. Money was the answer. It always was.

Jackie took him to one side. "It's not that simple," she murmured. "I've read about this sort of thing, you know. If Ron thinks he can find a cure, he's kidding himself."

She was wrong. She had to be. Jimmy had to do something. He couldn't let Tony die.

The club was deserted when Jimmy got back. He took a bottle of whiskey from the bar and settled down with it on the sofa. As if the sight of the hospital had been etched on to the inside of his eyelids, he saw that scene again every time he drifted off. Eventually, the booze knocked him out.

The dream began in darkness. Movement. Fast movement and the throbbing of a car. Jimmy knew he had to look where he was going, but his eyes were sealed shut. Then a bright, white, blinding light blasting into his face. Hands clenched on to the steering wheel. His right foot cramped and rigid, pressing the accelerator to the floor. He couldn't move, couldn't control what was happening. The speed was making him feel sick. Suddenly he was released. His vision cleared, his limbs were freed. Too late. Through the windscreen he could see the huge white car almost on top of him. Only it wasn't a roller. It was a hearse. In place of a coffin was Tony Dixon's bed. As they were about to collide, Tony sat up, ripping the tubes from his nose and wrists.

MURDERER

Jimmy woke up in a panic, heart beating so fast he could hardly draw breath, soaking the covers with sweat. He wanted to scream and scream till he'd blotted out his own existence. Only someone might hear, might find out.

Reaching for the mustard yellow envelope that never left his side, Jimmy tipped a small handful of coke into his palm. Not bothering with mirrors and neat lines, he snorted it. The relief was almost instantaneous. His pulse slowed, his head cleared and he could sleep.

Chapter 19

The worse Jimmy felt, the better people liked him. He threw himself into the Tony Appeal. Ron's desperation to find a cure for his son was nothing compared to Jimmy's. A charity night at La Luz raised a couple of hundred quid. Julia Brogan was persuaded to donate the funds from her annual Christmas Fayre. All the neighbours were rallying round. Everyone said how well Jimmy Corkhill was behaving. Turning over a new leaf, they said.

Jackie was touched by his kindness and Jimmy was allowed home. If only she knew. If only he could tell her. Ron was even worse. When he wasn't praising Jimmy to the skies, he was raging against the no-mark who'd been driving the other car. The one who'd put Tony in the hospital in the first place.

The Jiffy bag emptied. Jimmy could hardly believe he'd shoved three thousand pounds up his nose. Was he addicted? Brian always said it was impossible on coke. No. He wasn't hooked. He just needed something to help him through a rough patch. He'd gone beyond the stage where alcohol would do any good.

At least he knew where to score. The cabbies outside the club were only too happy to oblige. It was expensive, though. And risky.

Guilt made him careless. It was only a matter of time till he got caught.

Because he couldn't sleep at night, he developed the habit of taking coke, then catching forty winks in the office. One afternoon he was jerked awake by a shower of cola – poured by Barry Grant. In his hurry to get back behind the bar, Jimmy dropped a small, tell-tale plastic bag. Somehow he managed to convince him that it was a one off, like the incident with the ecstasy tab.

The pressure was taking its toll on his health. Ron called him a godsend. Jackie loved him. He was treasurer of the Tony Appeal – and the reason it was set up in the first place. Whatever else he'd been in his life, Jimmy had never been a hypocrite. He despised himself for taking the praise, but didn't know how to stop it.

It felt like he had a permanent cold. Psychological, that's what it was. His nose itched constantly. He wanted to sneeze, but nothing happened. And only coke could calm him down. When Tony was better, he'd stop. He promised himself that.

Tony was eventually moved to a general ward. The machines were taken away, so he just looked as though he was in a deep sleep. Above the bed was a sign: 'Remember The Patient Can HEAR' it said in big letters. It must mean something. There must be a grain of hope.

Ron had set his heart on Tony coming home for Christmas. Jimmy hated hearing him talk to the sleeping figure. The medical staff had said it could have a good effect, but it gave Jimmy the creeps. Like talking to a corpse.

The doctor called Ron into the nurses' station. There was bad news. A complication Tony had caught pneumonia. He'd be stuck in there for Christmas. And for the forseeable future.

"It's not fair," Ron wept. "It's not bloody fair."

That night, Jimmy spent two hours looking for a hit. It was

the only thing that relieved the pain. The stuff was miraculous. Jimmy's world had gone grey. Coke painted it in glorious technicolour again. Hope. That's what it gave him.

The best place to take it was in the bathroom. There was a small mirror in the bathroom cabinet that was perfect for forming lines. Perhaps Jimmy got blasé? Perhaps he wanted to be found out. One morning, he looked up and there was Jackie watching him.

"What're you doing?" At first, she was interested, rather than suspicious.

"Grass seed."

"What're you taking?" Her voice was rising.

"Nothing."

"Are you on drugs?"

What the hell did she think he was doing? Putting on his make up? Without thinking, he grabbed her arm and told her to get out. She lunged forward, snatching the coke out of his hand. The sound of the mirror smashing distracted Jimmy. Before he could stop her, Jackie had flushed twenty quid and a day's sanity down the loo.

"You stupid bitch." Jimmy shook her, squeezing her arms till he could feel bone. He was so angry, he could have carried on squeezing till the blood flowed. In despair, he threw her through the door and locked it.

He cowered in the corner, under the cistern, putting his hands over his ears to shut out the noise of Jackie screaming and swearing and hammering to be let in. Then, abruptly, she stopped. The quiet went on for hours before Jimmy could start to uncurl.

"Jimmy," Jackie said calmly. "Jimmy, please let me in. We've got to sort this thing out."

Cautiously, he opened the door to be confronted by a screaming harpie, all flailing arms and tearing fingernails. Crouched on the floor, he could do nothing but take it. One word kept repeating, through the accusations and insults and obscenities. Why? Why had he done it? Why did he need that filth?

"Because I can't take it."

By now, Jackie was exhausted, her anger spent. "Take what?" she asked. "For god's sake, Jim. Whatever it is, you shouldn't need drugs to get you through. Think of Ron Dixon. He's got a teenage son in a coma and he hasn't messed up like this."

What an example to choose. "Ron Dixon doesn't have to live with what I have to."

"What?"

"The guilt. The guilt of being the one who put his son in a coma. The guilt of putting Frank Rogers under a gravestone. It was me. It was me. It was me. I caused that crash. I killed the pair of them."

It was such a relief to hear it aloud. Jimmy broke down and sobbed, burying his head in Jackie's jumper. She held him until he could tell her the whole story.

"Everyone knows Frank was under the influence that day," she said when he'd finished. "How can you be so sure it wasn't down to him?"

"Because I was there."

He wanted to go to the police. Give himself the luxury of confession, punishment and redemption. Jackie wanted him to talk to someone. About the drugs.

"Are you a drug addict?" she asked him directly.

Jimmy started to deny it, but couldn't. "I don't know," he said. "I don't know what I am."

Now Jackie knew, life was easier and harder. Christmas was unbearable. Whilst on a high, Jimmy had persuaded Ron to hold a party in Tony's room. When the time came, he couldn't face it. Instead, Jackie made his excuses and left him to try and drink himself to oblivion. She didn't approve of that either.

"It's no use hiding behind the bottle," she said as she left.

She was right. Alcohol was useless. Jimmy reckoned even the dealers would be taking a break over Crimbo, so he didn't go out. He was up first thing Boxing Day, but it was difficult to get out of the house, with Jackie watching every move he made.

Before they'd seen in the New Year, Jackie had got hold of a load of leaflets. She took it all far too seriously. As far as she was concerned, he did a bit of coke, therefore he was a druggie. A coke head. Hopeless and lost. She didn't understand that he could stop at any time. If he wanted. It was just that, at the moment, he didn't want to.

Money was getting tight. At £20 a hit, coke was expensive and Jimmy's wages weren't as high as they had been. He couldn't cope with a lot of overtime. The ironic thing was that money passed through his hands the whole time.

Sinbad was joint treasurer with him of the Tony Appeal. It was his job to collect funds and put them in a building society account. People would give money to Jimmy to pass on. When Julia Brogan donated £50 from her pensioners, the temptation was too hard to resist.

Jimmy peeled off £30 and put the rest into the fund. It burned a hole in his pocket all day long, stopped him from scoring. He was on the rob again. Just as Jackie had predicted. And off Tony Dixon, of all people. It had to go back. Which still left him desperately short of cash. The till at La Luz was less personal. The bar maid got the blame when £50 went missing. Jimmy felt terrible about it, but what else could he do?

One of the stunts at the club had been a pile of pennies. They must have collected thousands. Bruce Grobelaar, the Liverpool goalie, agreed to push them over as a charity event. The club was packed that night. Ron was there, but even people's generosity couldn't lift his spirits. He sat with Jimmy and Jackie, the bucket of pennies in front of him, utterly in despair. The doctors wanted to stop Tony's life support. At first, Ron had resisted, but now he was starting to accept what they said. The thought of spending years visiting a son who was never going to improve was too much for him.

"Whenever I think about whoever was in that other car," he said, sounding as though he was talking to himself. "They're just walking free now, aren't they? Without a care in the world. Not knowing or caring that they've destroyed so many lives. If it wasn't for them, there'd be no need for any of this. How can they live with themselves? If I could just get my hands on them, I'd kill 'em."

There was nothing Jimmy or Jackie could say. With one sweep of his arm, Ron pushed the bucket of pennies off the table. Everyone looked round as the sound of coins jangling to the floor was heard for the second time that night.

"That's what I think of the money. It means sod all to me. It's not going to make our Tony any better, is it? All the money in the world won't save his life. It's over. I think it's only right that we let him rest in peace. Put him out of his misery."

All that money they'd raised and still no cure. Jimmy's mind went round and round, tormenting him until he could score. It was no worse than taking aspirin. Apart from being more expensive.

One afternoon, Mick asked him to keep an eye on the Pizza Parlour while he nipped out. No problem. It was dead quiet. You could hear a pin drop. Or the till ring. A few quid. Maybe Mick wouldn't notice. He'd think he'd made a mistake with change or the float or something. Jimmy slid nonchalantly behind the counter and opened the till.

At that moment, Sinbad walked in. He and Jimmy locked eyeballs.

"What were you doing with your hand in the till?" Sinbad asked.

"I didn't," Jimmy blustered.

"That isn't what it looked like from here. Why are you so strapped for cash? What're you playing at?"

It took hours for Jimmy to reach home that night. Jackie was waiting for him in the dark. Sinbad was with her, perched nervously on the edge of the sofa. They'd been discussing him and his so-called drug habit.

"OK. Alright. I admit it," Jimmy said. "I've been using coke. Occasionally. That doesn't make me addicted or anything.

"How do you know?" Jackie asked.

"Because I can take it or leave it. Look, it's not what you think. All sorts of people use coke. People you wouldn't expect. Doctors, brain surgeons, teachers. Educated people. People who wouldn't go near it if it was addictive or dangerous."

"And you think that makes it alright?"

"Why not? It's not exclusive to the middle classes, you know. If it's good enough for them, it's good enough for me."

Jackie's voice went hard. "Yes, but those sorts of people don't have to go robbing off their mates to pay for it, do they?" She started to cry. "Why? Why, Jimmy?"

"I'll tell you why." Jimmy was desperate for her to understand. "Because Ron Dixon's treating me like some bloody hero. It's all 'Uncle Jimmy' this and 'Uncle Jimmy' that. How d'you think that makes me feel, knowing what I've done? I've got to face Ron and DD nearly every day. Do you think I'd've been able to do that if it wasn't for the coke? I need it, Jackie. I can't get drunk any more. When I'm on it, I can hide from the world. That's all it does."

He knelt at her feet and took her hands in his. "I can't cope. I can't pretend that it didn't happen. I can't face anyone, because good old Jimmy is a nervous wreck. Good old Jimmy is a murderer. I killed a man. I put Tony Dixon in a coma. That's why I need it. I could stop taking it. I could give it up any time, but the fact of the matter is, I just don't want to."

Chapter 20

Tony Dixon died on a calm, cold February morning. In the end, he didn't need to be put out of his misery, he simply went by himself. Waves of grief flowed over the whole community as Ron rang round the neighbours.

When Jimmy heard he went into a state of shock. Although he'd been expecting the news, the reality hit him hard. He'd killed again. All his efforts to redeem himself, the obsessive fund raising, the nightmare visits to the hospital bed had been useless. He was the lowest of the low, a murdering druggie. There were no words bad enough to describe what he was.

The knowledge of what he'd done was like a physical ache in his chest. A pressure that wouldn't let him breathe, would hardly let him cry. After a day spent locked in the shadows of the bedroom, he was desperate to get out. The last thing he wanted was to show his face, but the urge to find something to relieve the pain was too intense to keep him in.

Jackie tried to stop him, planting herself between her husband and the outside world.

"Don't go out that door," she begged. "Don't go out that door, please."

"Frightened I might kill someone else?"

"I don't care about anyone else. It's you I'm frightened for. You don't need to take anything, Jimmy. You've got everything you need here. You've got me."

"I'm a scumbag, Jack. I don't deserve you."

"Well, you've got me. Like it or not, I'm sticking by you. And we're going to see this thing through together. Just the two of us. No drugs."

Why? Why did she have to be so good when all he wanted to do was die? After everything he'd put her through, she was still there. Jimmy couldn't push past her. Despair welled up inside him, pushing him down till he found himself collapsed on the stairs, wailing in Jackie's arms.

Ron came over later to ask if Jimmy would be a coffin bearer. Jimmy couldn't face him. Instead, he hid behind the door listening to him pour out his grief to Jackie.

"I feel as if I never even knew him properly. Me own son. Me own flesh and blood. What sort of a father am I, Jack?"

"A good one, Ron. You mustn't blame yourself."

"Why not? I'm the one that let him down."

"It was an accident. Somebody else caused that."

Somebody else. Her husband. Her cowardly, whinging, murdering husband cowering in the darkness. Jimmy couldn't live with himself. He slipped out to find relief.

"You look rough," his usual supplier commented.

Jimmy was beyond muttering more than a request for the usual.

"I think you need a bit more than that. Here. You smoke it."

The powder he handed this time was brown. Jimmy held out payment.

"Not this time, mate. Free trial. See how you get on. If you want more, there's a house two minutes away where you can get anything."

He whispered the address straight into Jimmy's memory.

Jimmy knew what he'd been given, knew how to use it. On automatic pilot, he found foil and a lighter and took his first hit of smack. There was no rush, no high. The first thing that happened was that he vomited. But it was as though his pain was no more than food poisoning. Once it was out of his system, the relief was instant. He could function again.

By the morning of Tony's funeral, Jimmy was sneaking off to the drug house almost daily. His mind was so clouded, he hardly noticed how quickly the habit had descended on him. All he could think of was his fear of the ceremony. The hushed voices, the community drawn together by grief. And in their midst, like Judas among the disciples, would be Jimmy, weeping with the rest, the cause of their suffering.

He had to go, had to do something. The smack would hold him upright for the morning. Jackie was pleased when he said he'd changed his mind. They changed into black and reached the chapel as everyone was going in.

When he saw them arrive, Ron came straight over and clutched at Jimmy. He was beyond words. It was time for the coffin to be lifted in. He couldn't refuse Ron's mute question. Stepping in behind him, he felt the coffin descend on to his right shoulder. Tony had only been a little lad, but Jimmy could hardly stand up under the weight.

The ritual wasn't too bad. Jimmy let the words wash over him. Ron's speech was harder to block out. The thank yous demanded to be heard.

"Special thanks to all the staff at the General. And especially two more guys. Sinbad, who organised Tony's collection, and Jimmy Corkhill, who's been there with us every step of the way. A true friend."

True friend.

True friend.

If only he had been a true friend. To anyone. He let everyone down. There was not one single person who hadn't been worse off for knowing Jimmy Corkhill. It should be him in that coffin. His funeral would have no mourners, no grief, no speeches. Let them shove him into the ground quickly and hold a party to celebrate ridding the world of a piece of evil.

Jimmy was brought back from his reverie by the congregation moving out to the grave. He was pushed to the front with the family. Was it really only six feet under they were burying the lad? It looked more like six miles. So deep. Buried under the weight of Jimmy's guilt.

The box of dirt was passed from hand to hand. First Ron, then D-D, then Mike. There was no sound except for the dull thud as earth met wood. Now it was Jimmy's turn to pay his last respects. How could he, knowing what he'd done?

Howling his shame, he sank to his knees, wishing he could fall into the grave. He cried to heaven for vengeance.

"No-one can help me."

"Jimmy, love." Jackie was by his side, trying to pull him up.

"Oh God. I'm scum. Tell him," he begged Jackie. "You've got to tell him."

"Tell me what?" Ron asked, bewildered.

"I confess. I killed your son."

"What?"

"I killed Tony. I was driving the other car. I caused the crash."

"You?" Months of rage went into that word.

Jimmy welcomed it. "I was tanked up to the eyeballs. I didn't know what I was doing."

Ron was too stunned to move. It was his remaining son who

sprang at Jimmy, aiming for his throat. The other mourners held him back, while Jackie dragged Jimmy to his feet.

"Get him out of my sight," Ron commanded. "Leave me to bury my son."

As soon as they were out of sight of the grave, Jimmy ran. Away from Jackie's pleading. Away from Ron's accusations. Away from himself. When his breath gave way he started to walk. He didn't know where he was. Some park. An isolated patch of green with no benches or swings. Only trees. Exhausted, he leant back against an oak, trying not to think.

Hours later, he became aware of a numbing cold. The wind was trying its best, but it couldn't match the chill of Jimmy's conscience. He had no money and no will to get enough to score a hit. His body craved relief and the relief had a form, a substance. A hot powder inhaled, more powerful, more necessary than oxygen.

His feet moved, shuffling, without the strength to pick up, put down a normal stride. A policeman came into view, speaking into his radio. For a moment, Jimmy panicked. Caught. Arrested. Charged. The uniform passed by.

That's what he had to do. Give himself up. Allow the forces of justice to punish and purge him. Now he could run. He had no direction and it was night by the time he reached the station.

"I wanna be arrested," he announced to the bloke behind the desk. "I wanna be locked up for life."

"Do you now, sir." The sergeant looked up from his paperwork. "Perhaps you could tell us why."

They took a statement. He told them everything. Every detail. It went down on the sheet. Then they said he could go. They'd be in touch.

"Is that it?" Jimmy was horrified. "Don't I go down? Aren't you going to press charges?"

"If we do, we'll let you know." The constable who'd taken his statement was impossibly young to be so fatherly. "Look, why don't you go home? Try not to worry."

Home. The word had no meaning. Patches of dark. Patches of light. Jimmy was aware of pavements receding to grass giving way to more pavements. Then bars. Railings. He was clutching at them as though he was in a prison cell. The cemetery was more than a jail, though. Much more for Tony Dixon. Jimmy could see the grave. The plain cross and the layers of flowers. Why couldn't they have been for him?

Guided by the spikes digging into his hands, Jimmy staggered to the gate. He knelt down and tried to pray to a god he'd never believed in. Couldn't believe in now.

A shadow fell over his face. D-D was standing over him, holding a wreath. White with orange blooms. He had no right to be there. What must she be thinking? But he was too weak to get up.

"You're the last person I expected to find here," she said.

"I was just . . ." Jimmy's voice trailed off.

D-D took in the funeral clothes, slimy with the grime of three days' wandering. She saw the hopelessness in his eyes.

"How long is it since you've had something to eat?"

Jimmy shrugged. Her compassion got the better of him and he found himself pouring out what had happened. How he'd gone to the police and they'd laughed at him.

D-D asked why he hadn't reported the accident at the time.

"I was scared and drugged," he confessed. "Drugged up on all kinds. I thought he'd get better. I was like you. I wanted him to go to Lourdes. I wanted a miracle. I can't tell you how sorry I am. I never meant any harm."

"He was a very kind boy, Tony." DD moved a bunch of lilies so her wreath could take pride of place. "He was always the first to help anyone."

"I'm sorry you found me here. Things are bad enough for you without me in your way. I'll get off." He tried to get to his feet.

"Where? Some back alley? Drugged up or drunk?"

"I'm sorry. I can't handle this." He had to escape from her sorrow.

"Jimmy. You need to get warm. You need some food inside you. I want you to come back to our house."

How could she say that after what he'd done? He tried to refuse, but she wouldn't take no for an answer.

"Why?" he asked.

"Because Tony would help anyone who needed it," she explained. "He was a kind lad,"

She helped him up and he leant on her as they made their way back to Brookside Close. Her children were disgusted by her actions.

"For the sake of our Tony's memory, I don't want anyone else hurt," she told them.

Soon Jimmy found himself warm, fed and watered. It hardly seemed to touch the chill he felt inside, but he was grateful. He'd always thought of D-D as a lumpy, sanctimonious woman. Her compassion astonished him. She really did have the strength to forgive.

Jimmy wouldn't let her phone Jackie. How could he face her after all the grief he'd given her, all the times he'd let her down? He had to go. D-D insisted he stayed. And had a wash. Plenty of hot water upstairs, she said.

Tony's room was next to the bathroom. Jimmy went inside

and sat on the bed. It was just like any normal fourteen-year-old's room. There was Dennis the Menace on the back of the door. Most of the walls were covered with Liverpool posters. Ron had kept up the league tables.

Above the desk Tony had put up snapshots. Reminders of holidays and outings in no particular order. A picture of Tony leaning back in his chair, grinning cheekily and putting two fingers up at the world caught Jimmy's eye. He'd been a bright, happy lad. Normal. Full of potential and he'd snatched it away. Again, the sluice gates opened and tears torrented. There was no end to them. How could there be, when he could never undo the damage he'd done.

The noise of coming and going from downstairs interrupted him. He looked over the bannisters. D-D had fetched Jackie. He'd never wanted to see her so much in his life, or wanted so much for her not to be there.

"Just go, Jack," he implored. He sounded like he was being strangled. "I'll only end up ruining your life as well as my own."

"Maybe. Maybe not. For better or worse. That's what we said, isn't it? I'm not leaving you like this."

Why was she doing it? Why couldn't she just leave him to his despair?

"Ever heard of St Jackie? Patron saint of lost causes?" she said, grinning in irony.

If ever there was a lost cause. Jimmy fell into her arms.

Chapter 21

There didn't seem to be much point in going to work. Even Oscar would balk at the way Jimmy had behaved, let alone Barry Grant. It was no surprise when the latter turned up at the house. He wanted to know if charges had been brought.

"No. Not yet," Jimmy said.

"So what's your plan then? Sit here and feel suicidal?"

Might as well get it over with, thought Jimmy. "Look," he said. "I know I've messed you around a lot. I'm sorry. As of today, I'll consider myself sacked."

"Just like that. You should hear yourself," Barry said scornfully. "Talk about wallowing in it. Listen to me, Jim. No one's arrested you yet. No one's sacked you. You've been carrying all this guilt round, but you've gotta keep going."

"Why?"

"Because you've got a wife. You've got a life. Worry about prison if and when they do you. If you can get yourself back to the club tonight, you've still got a job. It's up to you."

With that, he left. You could have knocked the Corkhills down with a feather. If he lived to be a hundred, Jimmy would never understand his boss. Maybe it was because they were almost family.

He wasn't fit for work. A shaking, tired barman was no use to man or beast. Promising himself it would be the last time, Jimmy pawned his watch to score.

It got him through the night. And the next. And the one after that. He pushed the worry to the back of his mind. It was like the coke, only cheaper. He just needed it to get through a difficult patch. When he was on his feet again, he'd stop. No problem.

Besides, he was going to get banged up anyway, so what did it matter? May as well be hung for a sheep as a lamb.

Getting a fix was easy. La Luz was so full of drugs it was a wonder the building didn't float. The drugs house was cheaper, but Jimmy needed an excuse to get to it. The guy who ran it, Macca, always offered the needle before handing over the usual dosage. It scared Jimmy. So far, he'd resisted the temptation. But it was a temptation nonetheless.

The world was shrinking. It boiled down to finding the money to buy the hit in order to feel normal. He didn't get high any more. Smack gave him relief, made him feel human. That was all. Without it, he shook, cramped and nauseated, till he couldn't pull a pint.

When she'd first found out about the drugs, Jackie had arranged for Jimmy's wages to be paid straight to her. Jimmy's old gambling habits had provided the perfect excuse. However, by this time Barry knew the truth. Jimmy struggled to survive. What Jackie allowed for pocket money scarcely lasted a morning.

Jimmy didn't want to go on the rob again, but he had no choice. It wasn't easy. His head was never quite clear and he seemed to have a permanent cold. Sometimes he looked at himself in the mirror and saw his hand scratching his nose when he hadn't been aware it was itching. The habit was automatic.

Not that he looked in the mirror too often. He wasn't a

pretty sight. Quite apart from the visible signs of ageing – the receding forehead and the advancing crows feet round the eyes – his lips were disfigured by cold sores and his skin had a góthic greenish tinge.

In his younger days, Jimmy had always regarded shoplifting as the housewife's choice of crime. It was too soft for him. There was none of the excitement of pulling off a scam or the glamour of robbing some posh jeweller's. Now he hadn't the energy for anything else. He couldn't concentrate for long enough to put a scam together. As for the bigger jobs, his hands shook too much. Besides, he was on the black list of every fence north of the Watford Gap.

He didn't even have enough nerve to knock off a few groceries. His first attempt was a farce. As soon as he got a side of smoked salmon tucked into his jacket, he caught the eye of a bloke in a green suit. The store detective. There was no mistaking the sharp look. Jimmy slid the fish back on to its shelf.

He was too humiliated to try again that day. Instead, he flogged his beloved leather jacket. Got three days' worth for it. He'd say it got nicked.

"You can't leave anything in that club," he told Jackie when she asked where it had got to.

She didn't believe a word. Eventually he had to confess that he'd sold it.

"For more of that stuff?" Jackie was winding herself into a rage. "I don't care how much it cost, it's going straight down the bog."

The threat was enough to unscramble his brains. The excuse was waiting for him. "I haven't got any stuff. I've kicked it," he said, using his most effective injured tone. "It's all gone. D'you know how much petrol that old banger of mine uses up, eh? Barry Grant doesn't give me anything towards it, you know. And I've got me dinners and that to buy. Just give us a few bob."

"I give you money every week," Jackie protested.

"Yeah. Like I'm some little kid. How do you think I feel, eh? Begging money from you? I don't like to ask. You've just gotta start trusting me."

She was always a sucker for guilt. Say anything that might imply she was doing something to damage their Relationship and she was putty. She handed him an extra tenner, believing him because she wanted to.

Her henchman, Sinbad, was acting like a nanny. Jimmy got sick of his anxious fat face poking its nose in all the time. What had it got to do with him anyway? He didn't have any idea what Jimmy was going through. To panic him, Jimmy swiped a batch of children's coats while he watched, horrified.

It wasn't enough. When his heroin reserves were low, his body and mind and personality took a dive. More and more often, he made the journey to Macca's. The house was purpose built, with blocked windows and peeling paint. It might have been nice once. Until the junkies moved in.

To gain entry you went round the back, skirting the piles of rubbish rotting in black bin bags. The pass word was Macca, but who he was, whether he actually existed, was anyone's guess.

Inside was a twilight world. The permanent semi-darkness was banded by slim strips of light spilling in through gaps in the boards. Around the walls, anonymous forms retreated into their private visions. No names. No faces. Cardboard and mattresses caught any fall-out. You got used to the smell of urine and vomit after a while.

He couldn't get enough by shoplifting. Luckily, not all houses were as well protected as Macca's. Somehow, when it came to watching out for likely targets, his vision became clear. The first job netted him enough for three days' supply. Again the needle was silently held out to him.

"I'll stick to me usual, thank you," Jimmy said, making his mouth form the words.

A pause, and the precious slip was handed over.

Why did he choose to rob Oscar's? Because it was familiar? Or because he knew the owner was in Spain? Perhaps. More and more, he resented anything well made and expensive. He'd had to give up coke for smack because he couldn't afford to keep up with the Smythes. Not that Oscar was posh. Far from it. But he was a have, where Jimmy was a have-not.

For such an astute man, Oscar didn't have much idea about security. The kitchen window was asking to be forced. Jimmy climbed through festoons of frilly curtains and stepped carefully into the sink. The gold taps provided a hand hold. Jumping down, he put his foot into a row of plant pots inexplicably set out on the floor. Him and his bloody green fingers.

It was a swift and easy job to fill a bag with ornaments and electronic gadgets. Oscar's taste was for the expensively ordinary. Nothing too unusual to alert suspicion. Just right for a thief. Jimmy was in and out of there in five minutes.

He left via the french windows into the garden. Might as well be civilised, he thought. Then the alarms went off. Two hungry young alsatians came bounding into view. Startled by their barking, Jimmy lost precious seconds dropping and retrieving his bag. By the time he reached the gate, he could feel the dogs' breath on his legs.

They chased him across the road to his car. Jimmy hurled

himself inside and drove off, saliva and scratch marks dis-figuring the side window.

When he heard what happened, Oscar asked Barry and Jimmy to check the damage and clear up the mess.

"Not very subtle, is it?" Barry said when he saw the broken kitchen window. "Oscar said sort out any damage. He's stuck in Spain for a couple of days. It's not worth cutting his trip short, just because some animal rips off a few bits and pieces."

"Yeah, well. He can afford it, can't he? No use in getting upset, is there?"

If Jimmy was looking for reassurance, he was out of luck.

"I didn't say that," said Barry. "You should have heard him on the phone. I wouldn't like to be whoever did this."

"Petty crime, isn't it? Chances are the police won't catch them."

"Yeah, but Oscar isn't just going to use the police, is he? He's got his contacts. He says he's going to find out who did it. He sounded dead serious to me. I feel sorry for whoever it was."

Did Barry suspect? He wasn't easy to read. Jimmy was on tenterhooks, especially when the bizzies contacted him to go down to the station.

He was to be charged with failing to report an accident. It was ludicrous. There was only one problem. Ron Dixon. He had threatened to kill his son's murderer. If there was no legal justice, he'd want his pound of flesh.

The ritual again. At Macca's, he asked for a fix to smoke. The needle was held out to him. Perhaps it stayed there a moment longer. Perhaps he was more desperate. Whatever the reason, Jimmy found himself reaching out for it. The props were all there – the spoon to hold the powder, the lighter to melt it, the check cloth to tie around the upper arm. The needle slipped into the artery like it belonged there. A sharp pain, relief, then the realisation that he'd gone too far.

Nausea rushed from his stomach, flooded through him. His body jerked, as though ropes tied to the back of his head and shoulders were being tugged hard. The movement made his head swim. The light patches across the floor were dwindling.

Shapes came and went across his field of vision. One solidified into anger. An impossible figure. Ron Dixon. How did he get there? Jimmy had just enough strength to lift his head. He tried to focus. It wasn't a nightmare. Ron really was in the room with him.

"I think I'm dying," he whispered.

"Rot in hell, Jimmy. You've saved me a job."

The last thing he saw was Ron lowering his arm. He'd got some kind of a weapon. Nemesis with a heavy duty spanner.

Chapter 22

For a long while Jimmy kept himself below consciousness. He didn't want to wake up. A world with him in it held no attractions. The people he'd damaged, let down and killed deserved better than that.

He was aware of Jackie's presence. Unsure whether he was seeing or hearing, he could feel her distress yanking him back. Through layers of cotton wool he started apologising, then opened his eyes. Her mascara had run, as it always did when she was upset, but the relief on her face was palpable.

When he was fully awake, she told him what had happened. Ron had called an ambulance, despite wishing him dead. He'd explained his reasons while they were waiting for Jimmy to come round.

"It was too easy," he'd said. "Why should he slip off when I had to carry on? He's stuck here, thinking about our Tony every ten minutes for the rest of his life. After all the grief he's caused me, I want to see him suffer. I want him to go on suffering for it. I wouldn't like to go through life with what that poor bugger's got on his conscience."

Survival would be Jimmy's punishment.

Being stuck in a hospital bed for a couple of days gave him a chance to think. The suicidal phase passed. Jackie was standing by him. Ron hadn't been able to hurt him in the end. The person he needed protection from was himself.

The nurses offered him something to make him sleep. He refused. Alone amid the grunts and snores of the general ward, he went over and over the past few weeks. He'd never been closer to death. If it hadn't been for the irony of Ron's arrival, he'd have been just another body heaved anonymously out of Macca's. Heroin kills. That's what the media said. For once, they were right.

While there's life, there's hope. Jimmy made up his mind. Whenever he was tempted to chase the dragon, he'd remember the terror of death and refuse. From now on, he was clean.

Jackie let him come home, but there were conditions.

"Look under the bed," she commanded.

He saw a couple of brown cases, bulging with clothes.

"Two packed suitcases, Jimmy. I put them there. So that the first time you lie to me, the first time you put any of that filthy stuff into your system again, I'm off."

She ticked the conditions off on her fingers. "No lies. No coke. No smack. And condition number four. You go to the drug counselling place."

Jimmy was appalled. He didn't want some trick cyclist telling him what to do. Now he'd made up his mind, he was off the stuff for good.

"I don't need counselling," he said angrily.

"Fine." Jackie picked up one of the suitcases. "I'll be at our Lindsey's."

There was no mistaking that look. Jimmy caved in, promising to make an appointment.

"It's alright," she said, pushing the case back under the bed. "I already have."

The atmosphere in the house was impossibly tense.

Neither could work out a way back to normality. Drugs over-hung everything – making tea, watching TV, washing up. Cups missed hands, smashed with twice their usual noise. Jimmy found himself chain smoking. His hands shook till he could barely use a match. He charred his fingers every time he lit a cigarette.

Jackie had been invited to a hen night. She didn't want to go. Jimmy persuaded her she should. He couldn't bear her constantly standing over him. It would do them both good. Perhaps he could relax when he was on his own.

"I'm not an invalid," he told her. "You think when you're out that door I'll get a fix, don't you? I won't. I swear. You can search me if you like. Jackie, you can't supervise me 24 hours a day. You've got to trust me. So go. Enjoy yourself."

Reluctantly, she left him to it. He meant what he said. Getting a tinnie from the fridge and the TV guide, he settled down for a quiet night in. There was nothing on. Restless, he went from sofa to chair to having a lie down on the bed. His palms were sweating and he couldn't keep still.

Fresh air. That's what he needed. He decided to go out for a paper. Walking, even with an object, didn't help. It was like he had an itch deep inside him, where he couldn't reach to scratch. Inevitably, his feet went in the direction of Macca's.

This was the last time. He promised himself that faithfully. It was only because Jackie was out and he was feeling a bit wobbly after hospital. Besides, there was the prospect of the bloody drugs clinic the next day.

The first shock was finding out that the counsellor was a tart. He would have walked out right then if Jackie hadn't reminded him of the two packed suitcases under the bed.

Faced with a powerful-looking woman with an ironed-out Woollie accent, Jimmy retreated into sulks.

"This was me wife's idea," he said.

The counsellor wasn't phased. "So basically, Mr Corkhill, you're saying we can't help you."

"Not me, no."

"Because you're not an addict. Is that right? You're not hooked? You can take it or leave it?"

"Yeah, that's right." Something about the way she said it made Jimmy uneasy. She definitely wasn't on his side.

"There's no problem because you control the drugs, they don't control you," she continued. "And the OD? It was just a one off, an accident."

"Yeah. It was." If she knew, why were they going through this charade?

Then she turned on him. "You see, Mr Corkhill, I'm word perfect. I know it off by heart. The number of times I've heard that. I've even said it myself."

"You were an addict?" Jackie said in disbelief. The contrast between Jimmy's battered appearance and this smart, almost elegant woman was stark.

"Ex-addict," the counsellor explained. "Not all of us are, but everyone is fully trained. We've seen the lot and we can help. We can even get you off the stuff, but you've got to want to first. You've got to really want to."

"He does," Jackie said before Jimmy could get a word in. "He does want it."

"No, Mrs Corkhill. That's what you want. He doesn't, because he's not an addict."

The woman was getting right up his nose. "I'm not staying here. It's a waste of time, love. There's no point."

Jackie tried to stop him walking out, but the counsellor seemed unconcerned. He started for home, angry with both of them. Then a vision of the two packed suitcases came into his mind. And somewhere, in a dark, hidden place, was the memory of last night's walk. He turned on his heel.

Jackie and the counsellor were still talking when he got back. They accepted his excuse that he wanted a breather. The counsellor asked him about the overdose again. He told her it was the first time he'd used a needle.

"That's not really the issue," she said. "The point is, however many times you used a needle, are you certain it was clean?"

"It was clean," Jimmy said. It had looked clean enough.

"No, I mean, are you absolutely one hundred per cent sure that no one could have used it before you."

There was a long, uncomfortable silence. "I don't know," Jimmy had to admit. "Someone just passed it to me."

"I don't want to panic you or anything, but I do think that both of you should arrange to have an HIV test." The counsellor looked worried. "As soon as possible."

Whether she had wanted to or not, the counsellor had panicked them. The thought of AIDS hadn't crossed their minds. For a week they argued back and forth. Jimmy was sure there was nothing wrong with him. He'd only used one needle once. The odds were so small as to be negligible. Weren't they?

Eventually Jackie lost patience when he refused point blank to get up for an appointment at the clinic.

"I'm not going for any test," he said from the depths of the bedclothes. "There's nothing wrong with me, alright?"

"You what? Taking all sorts of crap! Sticking needles in

your arm, like some divvy. You heard what the counsellor said. You could have caught AIDS. Now, you'll get yourself down to that clinic and find out about getting a test or I'll be getting those suitcases and you won't be seeing me again."

She insisted on coming with him. The waiting area was crowded. Jimmy looked around him, horrified. Most of the other patients were young, with the unhealthy pallor of a nocturnal life. Few could manage to sit properly, preferring to sprawl on the floor or perch on a chair with their arms hugging their knees. Instead of acne, their faces were marked by sores. The whole room seemed to be scratching and rubbing. The smell of the long-unwashed was nauseating.

Jimmy couldn't stay. He didn't belong there. Jackie rushed out after him.

"Have you looked in the mirror recently?" she snarled. "Seen the state of yourself? Because that's what you look like. Like that lot in there. You can't stand seeing the truth, can you? You're dirty and you smell. Your teeth, your clothes, your hair. Everything."

That hurt. Jimmy had always prided himself on his personal hygiene. He spent hours in the bathroom sprucing himself up. Reeking of Old Spice, he found Jackie in the kitchen. Her answering scent aroused him instantly. He put his arms round her waist and murmured into her ear.

"Here. Now. Like we used to. On the kitchen table."

She pushed him away.

"For God's sake! You shared a needle with some druggie." The disgust in her voice was unmistakable. "Get it into your head, will you? You could have AIDS. You've ruined your life. I'm not having you ruining mine."

It got into his head alright. From then on, he couldn't

think of anything else. Every waking moment, he was aware of his arm, aware of the place where the poison entered his bloodstream. He couldn't stop scratching and scratching till the inside of his elbow was a mass of scarred flesh. It was as if he could feel the virus multiplying round his system. No matter how much he washed, he couldn't cleanse himself. He had AIDS. He was dirt, scum, rotten through and through. And a coward to boot. If he wasn't so scared of dying, he'd have found the courage to kill himself.

He only knew one way to stop his head spinning, but he'd run out of funds again. The house he chose to rob was in a quiet avenue. It was a doddle to open the kitchen's sash windows. The owners must live in the dark ages. Still, at least the ornaments should be good for a few bob. Jimmy went systematically through the sitting room, clearing the mantelpiece and shelves of candlesticks, knick knacks and photo frames.

His normal method of exit was a cheeky stroll through the front door, but when he heard the key in the lock, he made an emergency dive back the way he'd come. Pulling himself through the window, he caught his hand on the jagged glass. Blood dripped into the solid, porcelain sink.

The cut was deep, but not serious. It was too awkward for Jimmy to bandage by himself, so he went to the Trading Post to ask Jackie for help. By that stage, he didn't care whether or not she believed his excuses about chopping carrots.

While she was fetching the first aid box, a customer came in with her infant son. Jimmy leaned over the carrycot. He put his hand out to give the lad a tickle, but was stopped by a yell from Jackie.

She said something and nothing about Jimmy spreading

germs from a cold, but after she'd finished serving she issued a warning.

"If you want to play with this baby or your own grand-child, you'd better take this bloody AIDS test."

Once again, he didn't have any choice.

Chapter 23

Two hours they kept him at Parkside Clinic. Two hours sitting in a room full of people waiting to see if they were going to snuff it. They were the same degenerates who'd been there to see the counsellor. Jimmy fixed his eyes firmly on a six inch square of lino, blanking them out. He didn't belong with them. No way. He wasn't a junkie. He could take it or leave it.

So why was he taking it?

By the time his name was called, he was a nervous wreck. One look at the state of him and they'd have hospitalised him for definite. A nurse took him into a cubbyhole and asked him if he'd had counselling.

"Yeah. That's why I'm here, isn't it? The tart told me I had to."

"So you understand the implications if the test should show you are HIV positive?"

"Yeah, yeah." Jimmy just wanted to get it over with. "Look. I don't wanna talk about it. Just tell me if I've got AIDS, will you?"

The test itself was nothing. A sample of blood and another age waiting for the result. Jimmy sat in the same seat, stared at the same tile.

"Mr. Corkhill? Would you like to come through."

The test was clear, but before Jimmy could relax, he was told he'd have to come back. Because he'd last injected only a few weeks ago, the virus might not show yet. He'd have to wait another two months.

It was doing his head in. Two months. How was he supposed to get through that? Jackie wouldn't even give him a cuddle until he'd been given the OK. He couldn't face the thought of two months like the last two weeks. Every waking moment he'd be worrying about it, scratching at his arm, convinced he was a walking cell culture. The same feeling as before, of evil multiplying in his bloodstream, crept over him. Then that urge for relief tugged him towards the mean streets.

No.

He was determined about one thing. He was off the smack for good. That's what got him into this mess in the first place. Take it or leave it. This time he was going to leave it, no matter what crap life threw at him.

Jackie was watching for him through the Trading Post's window. He was horrible to her and hated himself for doing it. It wasn't her fault, but if it hadn't been for her nagging he'd never have been told about the bloody test in the first place. He threw down the results like a gauntlet, then stormed out of the shop.

Immediately, he regretted it. What was he doing? Jackie was the one good thing in his life. She'd stood by him above and beyond the call of duty. He was too ashamed to go back and apologise.

Work entirely failed to take his mind off things. Unfortunately, he could unload bottles and wipe tables and still think. He concentrated on thinking of ways to make it up to

Jackie, trying to blot out the little voice whispering a cure to his agony.

Once more won't hurt, it persuaded. Just once, then you can give it up for ever. Only once, to make you feel human again.

Jimmy found himself shrugging his shoulders in an effort to get rid of the demon. How could he give Jackie a treat? Think of that. He had to find something active to do that didn't cost anything. What about making her tea? She'd love that, being waited on hand and foot.

Barry was more than willing to give him a couple of hours to prepare the great feast. If Grantie could be said to have a soft spot, it was for Jackie. He held out a couple of notes to pay for some flowers.

"That's flowers, Jimmy," he said as his barman left.

Jimmy meant to buy them. He'd been given enough for a substantial bunch. Before he could face going home, he had to have a walk to clear his head. He felt as if he was constantly wading through cotton wool these days. Somehow, the want, the need for heroin stole over him. It was a craving, much stronger than he'd ever had for alcohol. It wasn't pain, exactly, more a desperate lowness that made everything else seem completely insignificant.

There was enough left over after the fix for a few red roses. Jackie'd get her flowers and a husband fit enough to join the human race. The comfort of smack melted Jimmy's resolve. He'd try again another day, but for now he was just grateful for the feeling of normality.

It should have been a good evening. The meal turned out perfectly and they ate in front of the fire. As he put his knife and fork down, the familiar edginess started to invade Jimmy's system. It took the form of the AIDS test. That place on his arm itched unbearably.

"Leave it," said Jackie, taking his hand gently. "You'll get it infected."

"If it isn't already."

"Don't talk like that, please."

Jimmy apologised. "It's just I can't get this bloody AIDS test out of me head."

"There's no point in worrying yourself sick about it. You'll just have to wait."

As if logic had anything to do with it. He'd be in a strait jacket in two months.

"No you won't." Jackie stood up to go into the kitchen. "Anyway, it could do you a favour in the long run. All this worrying. It's enough to put anyone off drugs and needles for life."

Which showed what a lot she knew about it. The worry was driving him to the stuff, not away from it. He was like a cat on a hot tin roof, unable to keep still or get comfortable.

Jackie gave him a pep talk when he tried to explain how wound up he was.

"You're over the worst now, aren't you?"

"Maybe," Jimmy shrugged.

"Hey come on. Believe in yourself. You're not going to get back into those drugs again now. Not after all that's happened. Are you?"

"No. I'm not." He hated lying to her, but what else could he say?

He slipped off half an hour earlier than he needed to and went to work via Macca's.

Half the time he was desperate to fight his addiction, the other half he was desperate to give in to it. The word seeped into his brain. Try as he might to deny it, part of him was aware that he was hooked. The part of him that drove him to lie and hide and steal. The more he hated himself for doing it, the more he couldn't help it.

The thought that he had almost robbed a mate tormented him. Mick didn't deserve a no-mark like Jimmy for a friend. The Farnhams, however, were another matter. Their snotty middle-class accents and attitudes irritated the hell out of him. It would serve them right to have their house done over. If he'd had as much money as them, he would have been able to stick to cocaine, instead of heading downhill with smack. Besides, they'd be insured up to the hilt.

One good thing about living in a gossipy place was you got to hear when people went on holiday. Those that could afford it. Jimmy watched the Farnhams drive off and silently promised them he'd be round that evening.

Getting in was a doddle. No burglar alarms to worry about. Jimmy shone his torch around the living room. It illuminated the state-of-the-art stereo, with the stack of CDs beside it. Glass shelves held up by tubular black showed off discrete – ie. expensive – pieces of art. There was nothing here that you could label a knick knack. Even the kids' toys were designer. Max's briefcase was on the sofa. Jimmy opened it up. Mobile phone. Very nice. Very saleable.

Jimmy concentrated on small stuff, sweeping the lot into his bag. A kind of frenzy came over him and he found himself tearing the place apart. Whatever was too big to rob, he destroyed. Anger overwhelmed him. Up in the bedroom, he hurled clothes he couldn't sell across the floor, relishing the sound of ripping cloth. God, there was a lot of jewellery. Rings, brooches, necklaces. The works. People shouldn't be allowed to possess so much. It all went into the bag.

Outside again, panting with the effort, Jimmy felt cleansed. He'd grabbed enough to buy supplies for weeks. The jewellery was spread around the local pawnbrokers and he sold the rest of the stuff from the boot of his car. The haul netted him £1,500.

There was a funny side to it. Old David Crosbie, Patricia Farnham's father, marched up to him as he was sweeping up outside the club. The poor old buzzard was red in the face with accusations. Everyone knew about Jimmy's drug problem, therefore he must be the culprit.

"Look. If you burgled the place," he ended up, "just hand back the swag and no more will be said."

Jimmy put on his most injured air. Alright, he knew he was guilty, but it was still unfair that he was always first in the frame.

"I'm sick of people in this community pointing the finger," he said. "Mob rule, is it? I could lose me job, d'you know that? Yeah, I've had a drugs problem, but I'm finished with all that now. I've got me wife behind me, you know. And me boss. Alright it's a struggle, but I've been keeping me head above water. And now this. I know I'm worthless in your eyes, but I don't need kicking when I'm down."

The poor sod crawled off with his tail between his legs.

He did an even better job on Jackie. When she discovered the money in his jacket pocket, he thought the game was up, but the old charm and quick thinking were still working.

"You've robbed it to buy drugs, haven't you?" she said, waving a wad of notes under his nose. "God almighty. No wonder you've been so happy. You're still taking them. What is it now? Back to the cocaine?"

He could deny that in all honesty. Smack was the name of the game now. She demanded to know where the money had come from. There was a pause while Jimmy tried to get his head together.

"You've run out of lies," Jackie shouted. "You've lied and lied to me so often, you've run out of them. First, it was the dream house. Then the big business deal. Then you took me charm bracelet. Me charm bracelet that I had for fifteen years."

Inadvertently, she'd given him the hook he needed.

"Oh God. I wanted to keep it a secret," he said, using an agonised tone. "I got the money to buy back your charm bracelet. Yeah. I wanted it to be a surprise. I was going to buy back your bracelet. That's why I got the money."

"I want to know where you got this from."

Trust Jackie to stick to the point. But the ball was rolling and the lies simply fell out of his mouth.

"I borrowed it," he said. "This bloke in the club does personal loans."

"A loan shark? Oh God, Jimmy, you'll never pay this much back."

"It's personal terms, love. It's just a few percent interest on thirty quid a week for 36 months. Less, if I pay a bit more a week."

Jackie implored him to return the money. Suddenly Jimmy realised he wanted more than anything to get her bracelet for her. It was so important to her, he had to do it.

"It means a fresh start. For you and me," he explained. "If you'll just give me a bit more out of me wages each week, enough to pay off the loan, I'm happy."

It was as if the loan really existed, conjured up out of his imagination. Eventually, he convinced her and had almost convinced himself that he wouldn't spend the extra on drugs.

"Trust me, love," he said, hating himself because she would.

Chapter 24

Jimmy's satisfaction at getting Jackie's bracelet back was tempered by his need for money. The tiny bit extra he was allowed from his wages barely saw him through a day. A new family had moved into Brookside Close. They seemed alright, but they weren't mates or anything. Which made them fair game. Again, he'd overheard one of them talking in the Trading Post and discovered when the place would be empty.

Only they weren't as organised as the Farnhams. The woman came back as Jimmy was rummaging through her knicker drawer. Pushing past her, he made a dash for the front door and ran straight into her husband, coming in to fetch his wallet.

They had no qualms about handing Jimmy over to the police. Suddenly, he was caught up in the heavy treadwheel of the authorities, given a solicitor and brought before the magistrate. There was no hiding what he was and what he'd done now.

Jimmy couldn't afford a posh brief with a wig and a grand manner. He had to make do with the dregs of a big firm, seeing anyone who happened to have a moment free. After his arrest, he had a talk with one bloke, who told him to plead guilty and mention the drugs habit. It would also be a good idea to ask for the other burglaries to be taken into consideration.

This was unnerving enough, but when Jimmy was faced with a sandy haired, chinless stranger two minutes before they went in, his confidence plummeted still further. Jackie squeezed his arm and looked worried.

"I'm Martin Glennister. You spoke to my colleague, I believe," the bloke said trying to shake hands and cling on to a stack of papers at the same time. "Listen. We haven't got much time. They went through like the clappers this morning. Right." He fumbled through the file. "So it's, er, burglary, yeah?"

Oh, this guy really knew what he was doing. He kept sneezing as well.

"I've got a rotten cold," he excused himself. "Well, I gather my colleague's advised you to plead guilty. It's your best chance and we're asking for mitigating circumstances to be taken into account."

"What sort?" Jackie asked.

"I was thinking of your husband's drug habit. If the magistrates know your husband was burgling in order to get money for drugs. . . ."

"Won't that count against him?"

"No. We might swing it to our advantage. Don't worry, Mrs Corkhill." He blew his nose again. "And one other thing, you do know we're asking for other offences to be taken into account."

As it happened, she didn't. Jimmy hadn't meant her to find out this way, but there hadn't been a right time to tell her about his other little jobs. Her fury would have to wait, they were being called in.

Stealing a look at Jackie, stony faced in the public gallery, Jimmy would have welcomed being remanded in custody, but he was awarded bail. A probation officer would be detailed to make a report for the sentencing hearing. Next available date after three weeks. The gavel came down and Jimmy had to leave the dock to face his wife.

"I want dates. I want times." Jackie turned on him as soon as the brief had dashed off. It took Jimmy half the bus ride home to make a clean breast of it. The other half was spent in silence.

"You were robbing off our neighbours to feed your habit. Is that right?" Jackie started again as soon as they were in the door.

For form's sake, Jimmy protested his innocence, although he realised he'd lost her for good this time. She was sick of sitting around all night scared stiff he was out on the rob again. He could promise he was off the stuff till he was blue in the face. It wouldn't wash any more.

"You swear that now," she said bitterly. "But the next time you're desperate for a fix, you won't care what you sell. You'll be on the rob again. I'm not having it Jim. I'm not gonna let drugs rule me life."

She dragged the two packed suitcases from under the bed. It was no dramatic gesture. He'd lost her.

"I'm sorry for what I've put you through. I don't know how you've had the guts to stay so long," he said quietly. "I don't blame you. You should have walked out months ago. I'll miss you, Jack."

At the door, she kissed him on the cheek, told him to look after himself. She would be at Lindsey's. The door closed behind her. Jimmy stared at the featureless wood, a chasm of loneliness opening up to swallow him. He'd do anything to get her back. In one moment, he'd silently promised to give up the smack, go to the drugs counsellor, hold down his job, be a good father and husband, if only he could be allowed one final chance.

As if there was a God, the door opened slowly. Dulled by defeat, Jackie walked back in. Whatever it was between them, the years of battling against Jimmy's turbulence, the sparks of rage and love, it was still tying them together.

"Take my cases back upstairs," she said. "I'll unpack later."

Knowing how near he'd come to losing her for good, Jimmy then found himself holding his breath around the house. If Jackie had to go in to work early, his mind leapt to the conclusion that she wasn't coming back. It was the kind of thing he knew he was capable of, even if he was just as sure Jackie wasn't. Still, he needed her spoken, solemn oath. Again, there was the relief as she vowed. And the pain like a knife. Like a needle.

Unbelievably, he still had a job as well. Instead of sacking him, Barry demoted him to general dogsbody. He even said he'd write a reference for the court. But there were the long afternoon hours to get through, with only daytime TV to keep him company.

Without the smack to keep him normal, Jimmy had the constant sensation of falling into an abyss. The horror was shapeless, a black nothing threatening to engulf him. He couldn't cope. He might as well admit it to himself.

Prison terrified him. How could that pathetic divvy keep him out? If he could have afforded a proper brief, there might have been a chance. His background, his accent, everything was against him.

With everything laid bare, why try to get off the stuff? Once he'd gone down he'd have to stop. Maybe it would be for the best. Jimmy started to strip the house systematically of its assets. After the months of fighting and denying his addiction, it was so much easier to just give in. Admit it.

The probation officer came round. He was as humourless as a robot. Everything he said sounded like he was reading a police caution. Jimmy found himself staring at his repulsive, thick lips, moist with saliva. He was aware that his gaze was not returned. In fact, the fella seemed to block out the bags under the eyes, the pallor and the cold sores disfiguring his mouth.

Jackie's anxiety was making her over helpful. Jimmy hated that, hearing her kowtow to this ponce. It made him bolshie. He couldn't even bring himself to sit down.

The probation officer got out his clipboard. Stage one, introduce self. "I'm Paul Heery," he said, speaking slowly and carefully. "I'm the probation officer assigned to your case. Before you start, do you want me to explain how this works?"

"Not bothered," he shrugged. Just get on with it, he added silently.

Tick on the clipboard. Stage two. "Now that Mr Corkhill has pleaded guilty to the charges against him, it's my job to do a report to the magistrates so that they can decide on an appropriate sentence."

"Is he going to go to prison?" Jackie asked.

"That's not for me to say." There were no instructions in his guidance manual for showing any sympathy.

"What if I want to go to prison?"

Paul Heery didn't react. "Do you want that statement included in my report? I can put it in," he said. "Now, if we could just take the specific count of burglary you were charged with. It was a drug related crime?"

Tick.

"Committed in order to finance a drug habit?"

Another tick.

"Was it carried out while under the influence of drugs?"

"No."

"Or while experiencing withdrawal symptoms from the drug?"

"Yeah. Yeah, yeah it was." He didn't need to rob while he was feeling OK. It was only when the smack wore off that he got desperate.

"And it was one of a series of crimes committed to serve your addiction."

The official starkness of the words hurt.

"Mr Corkhill?" Heery prompted.

"Yeah," Jimmy admitted, his belligerence finding a voice again. "Yes. I went on the rob because I'm a junkie, OK?"

"Could you possibly tell me what, if any, steps you've taken to combat your addiction?" Nothing could deflect this machine from his task. Jimmy retreated into silence.

Jackie spoke up for him. "We've been to see a drugs counsellor, haven't we, Jim?"

"So are you currently embarked on an ongoing drugs rehabilitation programme?"

"Not exactly."

"So when did you last seek help?"

"It was a while ago. We keep meaning to go back, don't we?" Her strained, ingratiating half smile infuriated Jimmy.

"Don't lie to him," he snarled.

Ignoring the outburst, Heery continued to follow his script.

"Under the circumstances, the resumption of some sort of treatment prior to sentencing can only help your case," he said.

"We will," Jackie promised. "We'll go back in the next few days, won't we, Jim?"

"I need Mr Corkhill's guarantee on that."

He agreed. For her sake.

"There is one more major question I have to ask. And I want you to think very carefully before answering," the probation officer said, emphasising each word till they were almost meaningless. "Bearing in mind all this information has to be passed on to the courts. If you do receive a non-custodial sentence, either community work or probation or rehab, do you think it's likely that you will re-offend?"

Jimmy could feel Jackie willing him to deny it. After so many years of lies, why start telling the truth now? Into his mind flashed a vision of safety. Whatever else they might do to him inside, they'd get him off the drugs.

"Yes," he answered clearly. "Definitely."

When they were alone again, Jackie tried to comfort him. He desperately wanted her to understand, desperately wanted her to leave him alone with his need.

"He did make a lot of sense," she said. "Especially about going the drugs clinic. If you had proper treatment he could keep you out of prison. You will go the clinic, won't you?"

"Have I got a choice?"

"Not really, love, no."

She pestered him to find out why he'd done it, robbing off his mates, stealing from his neighbours. There was a huge barrier between them, labelled smack. In a perverse way, Jimmy almost wished she was hooked too, so she'd know how it felt. She actually asked him if he'd been going 'wild turkey' when he'd been burgling.

Cold turkey. The expression was 'cold turkey'. A couple of

hours after the probation officer had left, she discovered what it was all about.

So did Jimmy. Because of Heery's visit, he'd managed to skip his morning fix. More often than not, he'd score in the afternoon to prepare him for work. The strain of the interview made it worse. It was months since he'd denied himself for this long. Soon his body was demanding that he feed his habit.

It started with the shakes. From extremities in towards the heart, Jimmy lost control to hot pulses of shivering. Jackie put her arms round him, trying to offer comfort. He was in no condition to explain to her that it was useless. She couldn't reach him in this state. Only smack could.

His stomach heaved and vomit burst out of him, filling the room with stink. It wouldn't stop. Never. Not till he got a hit. He begged Jackie to help him, to give him one lousy tenner. One more dose and he'd do anything for her, throw himself off a cliff, cut his wrists. Anything. Just save him.

Jackie backed off, horrified. Jimmy staggered after her, past her, into the garden. Sheets hung from the clothes line, blocking his way. He blundered into them and span to the ground, howling his agony.

"Shut up," Jackie screamed, repulsed by the nakedness of his need. "Can't you just shut up? Can't you see you're killing yourself and dragging me down with you?"

Why wouldn't she understand? He knew exactly what was happening, but he was powerless to do anything about it.

Chapter 25

Cajoled, nagged, pushed and prodded by Jackie, Jimmy made it to the clinic the next day. The counsellor droned on about God knows what. Jimmy tried to give the right replies. Yes, he really wanted to get off the stuff. Yes, he had the full support of his wife. Yes, he would make a commitment to stay away from the smack.

His reward was a prescription for methadone. It would ease his symptoms, came in controlled quantities and was legal. A wonder drug, in other words. The arguments went over his head. Substituting one drug for another didn't make much sense to him, but he had to go through with it, for Jackie's sake.

The bottle was tiny. As soon as they were through the door, Jimmy ripped the top off and knocked about half of it back before Jackie managed to snatch it away.

"One capful three times a day," she read off the label. "You just swigged your ration for the whole week."

"Don't be soft. Give us it."

"You haven't given up the other muck just to kill yourself on this stuff." Jackie had gone into bossy mode. "One capful. Three times a day. This isn't just some new drug, you know, you can get high on. It's supposed to help you give the other stuff up."

"Yes sir, no sir, three bags full."

She was worse than that bird down the clinic. Nagging and humiliating him to keep him in line. Jimmy hated being told what to do. Resentment welled up inside him, insisting that he rebel.

The dose was too low in any case. Within an hour of taking his one pathetic capful, he was craving again. He kept the bottle in his pocket like a talisman. Three days later, it was empty.

He had no choice. Somehow, he had to score. The promises and the threats meant nothing compared to his need. It drove his hands into Jackie's coat pocket, looking for money. He found 30p. So now she was keeping her money away from him.

Like a little kid making excuses to his teacher, he pretended he'd broken the bottle. Of course, she wanted to check, wanted to see the pieces of glass for herself.

"I thought all this was gonna be based on trust," he said, putting on his most injured tone. Then he begged her for money to get some more.

"What're you talking about? You get it off prescription," she replied.

"I can't. They ration it. I only get one prescription a week."

"Just tell them it was an accident. You dropped it."

"You really think they're gonna believe me? A druggie." Jimmy could hardly believe how naive she was. "I know someone who sells it. Can I have the money?"

"I'll go to the drugs clinic with you. I'll sit up all night with you. Anything, but I can't give you money."

Fat lot of use she was. "So I've gotta suffer then?" he said.

"Keep your mind occupied. Push the drugs out your head. You can do it. It's just will power."

Just will power! She had no idea. As far as she was concerned, it was as easy as resisting a piece of chocolate cake. Left alone while she smarmed to customers in the Trading Post, he paced through the house, unable to read or watch or listen. Keep his mind occupied? It was occupied already. Invaded by smack.

He had to find her. The choice was simple.

"Look at me," he demanded. "I can't do without the methadone. D'you really think I can wait for some crappy prescription. I can't. I can't do without it."

"Try." She wouldn't take in his hair, lank with sweat, or his desperate, trembling mouth, aching from sores.

"What you're asking me to do is impossible," he begged. "Right. You know what I've gotta do, don't you? I've got to go out there and steal, because that's the only way I can get the stuff. And rather than give me twenty lousy quid for a bottle of methadone, you'd sooner see me go on the rob again."

Silently, she pulled out two tenners and handed them over. He promised her he'd buy methadone and be a good little boy next time. Good old Jackie. He knew she'd come through for him in the end.

He meant to buy methadone. He really did, but the first place he tried didn't have any. Too done-in to go anywhere else, he bought his usual amount of smack. The hit was so good, it was almost worth being deprived of it for a week.

Jackie found him back home, relaxed and happy, listening to the stereo. She picked up the tell-tale paper and rounded on him.

"You were suffering, remember?" she said.

"Who's suffering?"

"You got smack. You were supposed to get methadone."

"It's my life. Jackie. Smack," he said, enjoying her discomfort. "I'm into it. I burn for the stuff. I'm a junkie. This is what junkies do. You're married to one." He put on a mock romantic, sing song voice. "You gave me the money 'cos you love me."

Did she understand now? Her face was ashen with shock, so perhaps she did.

He loathed himself when he'd come down a bit. You always hurt the one you love. That was how the saying went, wasn't it? They were locked into this, the two of them. He hadn't wanted to involve her. It was somebody else doing all these horrible things to her. Some no-mark on smack.

When his head was clear, on a rare good day, he thought he didn't need it any more. Seeing what drugs had done to the two of them, he wanted to pack it in. Then the craving came over him and he had no way of controlling himself.

Jackie constantly checked up on him. If he spent more than two minutes reading the paper on the bog, she was tapping on the door. It irritated Jimmy immensely, especially when she got Sinbad doing the same around the club.

The worst moment happened in public. Jimmy was in La Luz, trying his best to ignore his body. He shifted crates and wiped tables, while panic rose in bubbles from his stomach. It shot out of him as vomit three times in an hour.

Why fight it? Who cared what the neighbours thought? Barry, Sinbad, Jackie. They could all join him in hell. His whole world had narrowed down to a square of paper and a teaspoon of brown powder.

Jackie would help him, though. She was his missis. Always came through for him. He dragged her out of the shop, demanding twenty quid. If she didn't give him it, he'd be forced to knock some old granny over the head. She cried, she shouted, she pleaded, but she wouldn't hand it over.

There was a kid's bike leaning up against a lamp post. Jimmy grabbed it. It was in good nick. He'd get the money for a hit, easily. Sell the bike or get it from Jackie. By now, he couldn't give a toss which it was.

Jackie's terror meant nothing to him. The notes she took out of her purse did.

"I knew you'd come good for me," he told her.

There were only three days till his court hearing. Three days of freedom. He was going down, no doubt about it. Might as well make the most of the time he had left. The night before, he didn't come home at all.

Exhausted, he staggered back as everyone was going off to work. He collapsed into bed and would have been asleep immediately if Jackie hadn't kept shaking him. They had to go, now. Summoning up his last ounce of strength, he pushed her away. She was much lighter than he'd expected and landed with a crash on the other side of the room. Unconsciousness overtook him before he had time to regret what he'd done.

Icy water on his face woke him up. Sinbad was standing over him, cup in hand.

"Come on, you. Out of bed."

Jimmy opened his eyes, he wasn't accustomed to seeing Sinbad like this. Then he realised what must have been going on.

"Oh, I get it," he said. "You and Jackie, eh? Comforting her, while her junkie husband goes out on the razz."

"Don't be a divvy," Sinbad replied. "Just get your clothes on."

Jimmy managed to make himself upright so he could attack his wife's lover, but he found himself sprawling on the bed, with his jaw aching from where Sinbad had punched him. The shock woke him up completely. He saw the fat fella blowing on his knuckles and a wave of shame came over him. Like a lamb, he dressed himself as smartly as he could. His suit had long gone, and he had to make do with almost clean jeans.

As usual, they had to wait ages at the court. Jimmy was parched. His mouth was worse than a parrot's cage. Sinbad fetched hot, sweet tea, as though he'd been in an accident. He was in a state of shock, if truth be known. What would have happened if he hadn't got out of bed? It would have been squad cars and bizzies and god knows what. They'd have banged him up and thrown away the key.

Awkwardly, he apologised to Sinbad. "About time someone knocked some sense into me," he said. Knowing he was going down, he asked Sinbad to take care of Jackie for him.

"The only place you're going is that pub across the road," Sinbad tried to reassure him, but the words picked up the echo from the high ceiling.

Jimmy had no words to tell Jackie how he felt. Sorry was pathetic. He'd said it so many times it had stopped meaning anything. All he could do was look at her. This was the end for them. Understanding at last, she put her arms round him and they hugged until they were called into court.

As he was shut into the dock, Jimmy glanced at the bench. Some tart was in the middle. That didn't bode well. Women in authority were always more vicious in his experience. A white haired old fart sat on her left and a young one in a toupee on her right. None of their faces moved as Martin Glennister spoke in his defence.

To do him credit, he did a good job. He said all the right things about doing the jobs to feed a drug habit.

"An addiction which he has now recognised and for which he intends to seek help by enrolling on a recognised drug rehabilitation programme," he said. In other words, Jimmy had promised to go down the clinic.

"This programme will not be available to Mr Corkhill if the court passes a custodial sentence. I recognise it is the duty of the court to protect society against crime. However, it is in the interests of not only Mr Corkhill, but of the community as a whole that he is given the opportunity to enrol on the programme, as failure to kick the habit will mean the defendant inevitably reoffends." In other words, if he was banged up, he'd end up doing it again.

Barry's reference went down well, as did Jackie's promise to help him pull through. Even the police helped, saying Jimmy had been co-operative.

"Taking all these things together," Glennister concluded, "I would ask for the court to exercise leniency in giving Mr Corkhill a *non*-custodial sentence."

Jimmy saw Jackie and Sinbad exchange a relieved look. Perhaps they'd be buying the solicitor a drink as well.

There was another wait while the magistrates conferred. As soon as they were let back in, Jimmy knew there was no hope. None of the three would look in his direction. They'd ganged up on him.

The old bitch dismissed all the arguments in Jimmy's favour. The one thing that mattered was that he'd dared to deprive the rich of some of their possessions.

"Burglary is not only a crime against property, it is a crime which causes a great deal of anxiety and insecurity in the community," she intoned. "In a civilised society, the public should feel safe and secure in their homes. It deprives the victim of that sense of safety and security and, as such, is a crime of the utmost gravity, which cannot be tolerated. It is the duty of this court to protect the public from such crimes and in considering the sentence to be passed, it is also the duty of the court to deter other potential offenders. For these reasons, I have no alternative but to pass a custodial sentence. You will be sent to prison for nine months, with a recommendation that you attend the prison hospital for treatment for your drug addiction."

Raising her voice to be heard over Jimmy's desperate cries for his wife, she ordered the officers to take him down.

Chapter 26

As soon as he could, Jimmy sent a visiting order to Barry. He couldn't face Jackie or even Sinbad seeing him in this state, but he had to see someone. Somewhat to his surprise, Barry showed up. He offered to bring Jackie down.

Jimmy refused. "I don't want to see her. Not till afterwards. If she's still around, that is. She's entitled to a life. She shouldn't feel as if she's tied to me. Tied to what? A bloody wreck. A junkie."

"So you're just going to dump her," said Barry. "After she's stood by you. Well, she wants to see you."

"I won't send her a visiting order." Jimmy had thought long and hard about it. "I've gotta let her have a chance. I don't want to lose her either, but it's me own fault. And it's no more than I deserve."

Back in his cell, he sank into darkness. The next four weeks were a blank. Not knowing the ropes and feeling too ill to find out, he didn't get to the prison hospital. Instead, he shivered and shook in his bunk, marking time by the waves of stomach cramps, punctuated by lights on, lights off. The screws left him alone. As long as he was quiet, they weren't bothered.

It was like three heavy doses of flu piling on top of one another. Then, as if he really did have flu, he started to recover. One day, he realised he'd been in a month. He was awake enough to be aware of the grey walls, the sagging discomfort of his bed, the inadequacies of the blankets and the indignity of the toilet.

Most of all, he was aware of what he'd done to Jackie. He missed her desperately, far more than he had when she'd chucked him out. The thought had always been at the back of his mind that there was a chance for them to get back together. What had he got to offer her now? He loved her too much to want her to stay involved with a scumbag like him.

Every night he lay awake, torturing himself with the thought of Jackie with another man, imagining them in bed together. Whoever he was, he wanted to kill him. Then he'd realise that another man would be the best thing that could ever happen to her. Someone who'd treat her properly. Someone who'd realise how special she was. He loved her, but he was no good for her. Never had been.

There was a snapshot of her and the kids above his bunk. Her smile encouraged him to become a model prisoner. The dull routine made it quite easy. Little was demanded of him and he got brownie points for the tiniest evidence of co-operation.

He was assigned work in the laundry. Not the most prestigious job, but it got him out of the cell. Whatever he did, he kept Jackie at the front of his mind. Soon she'd replaced smack completely.

But he still couldn't bear to see her. On the one hand, he was foaming with jealousy at the thought of her cut loose from him. On the other, he wanted the best for her, which meant letting her go.

Sinbad proved to be a lifeline, visiting every couple of weeks. He gave the lowdown on all the gossip from Brookside, including news of Jackie.

"She doesn't look half as tired as she did do," he reported. "Have you got a message for her? There must be something you want me to say."

"No. I just wanna know she's OK, that's all." There were so many things he wanted to tell her, but he didn't know how. "So any fellas hanging round then?"

He tried to sound casual. Sinbad wasn't fooled.

"No, Jimmy. What do you think?" he said.

"She's a beautiful woman, my Jackie. She still turns heads, you know. Loads of fellas would be queuing up for her if they knew she was free."

"Come on. You know Jackie. She's not gonna look at another bloke," Sinbad said. "If you're that worried about her, why won't you send her a visiting order?" He leaned over the table, as if he was about to reveal some great secret. "See her," he urged. "She's desperate to see you."

It was no use. He still couldn't bear for her to witness him inside.

His loneliness was eased when a new cellmate settled in. Don Macatyre looked hard. A big Scottish lad, broad shouldered and tatooed. However, the two men soon discovered they had a lot in common. Don might look like he held up Group 4 vans with his bare hands, but he'd been done for shoplifting. Thirty other offences to be taken into consideration. Mitigating circumstances? Feeding his habit.

Don had a passion for draughts. His set was never out of his sight. He wasn't much cop, though. Jimmy beat him easily. However, it soon became clear why he was so fond of the game. Tucked under the board were several familiar folds of paper.

"This should keep us happy," Don commented.

Determined not to break his resolve, Jimmy refused. Even seeing Don relaxed and mellow wasn't enough to make him give in. It would get easier, surely.

Don and Jimmy were both assigned to kitchen duties. The bustle was cheering and they even got paid – a colossal £9 per week. Jimmy saved every penny for his release. With good behaviour, he'd be out on parole in no time. As much as he tried to tell himself Jackie could no longer be part of his life, there was a hot flicker of hope encouraging him to think that maybe, if he could get his head together, she might take him back one last time.

Sinbad gave him a right laugh. He'd done his back in and had been ordered to wear a corset. Who'd have thought old Sin would have been a cross dresser? The best thing was that everyone knew. Someone had let the secret out down the pub.

"Your Jackie was there," he said. "Good to see her out and about."

Suddenly, the situation wasn't funny.

"My Jackie? Who else was there?"

Sinbad reeled off the names of several women.

"That's it? No fellas or anything?" Jimmy was fidgetting with insecurity.

"No. Only me. Why?"

"I just don't like the idea of Jackie going to pubs while I'm stuck in here." Even as he said it, he knew he was being unreasonable.

"Come off it, Jimmy," Sinbad protested. "What d'you expect her to do? Sit in the house crying about you all day? You won't even let her come and visit. You should be glad she's out enjoying herself. You're the one that's in prison, you know. Not her."

It didn't matter that Sinbad was right. Jimmy couldn't keep still. He'd developed an exercise routine, press ups and stomach curls. He went through it over and over again, trying to blot out the thought of Jackie copping off with some bloke.

Don tried to calm him down. His philosophy was that you couldn't do anything about the inevitable.

"If she wants to cop off with other people, she will," he said. "Makes no difference if you're in here or not."

Jimmy took a breather. "So it doesn't bother you?" he asked. "The thought of your bird out there while you're locked up in here?"

"I wouldn't blame her if she did cop off with somebody else. I know if things were the other way round I wouldn't be sitting at home every night twiddling me thumbs."

"So you wouldn't mind her sleeping with someone else?"

"Of course I'd mind, but I know I'd have to be realistic." Don reached for his draughts set. "If she sleeps with other people, I'd have to appreciate it's for sex, nothing else. If I think about it that way, I can handle it. I know she loves me. I know she'll be waiting for me when I get out. I can't expect her to lead the life of a nun in the meantime."

It wouldn't do for Jimmy. "If I thought my Jackie was carrying on with someone else, that'd be it. I just wanna get out of here. I'd escape if I could."

"Cool it. I'm telling you, man. There's only one way of escaping this mess."

"Smack, you mean?"

"Why not? It'll stop you tearing your hair out. I'm gonna have a hit. You're welcome to join me."

Jimmy refused. "It's because of that stuff that I'm in here and Jackie's out there."

"Yeah. At least this stuff'll help you forget what she might be doing. Go on, man. Take it. You know it makes sense."

Don made up the gear in the toilet. He came out with enough smokes to see them through the night and there were still loads left over.

"What are you going to do with that lot?" Jimmy asked.

"Stash it."

"Where?"

"Not here. The screws are always turning the cells over. I've got a little hidey hole for this lot where no one will find it."

At work, Jimmy watched Don balance the packet carefully on the inside of an extractor fan. It was never used, so there was no danger of the stuff being sucked up.

As soon as their work duty was over, the smack came out. Jimmy longed for just one hit, to feel good one last time. Don encouraged him.

"Go on, don't spoil the party," he urged. "This stuff's brilliant. I know you want it. It's written all over your face. Forget your troubles. Forget you're stuck in this place."

"I don't know," Jimmy said.

"I don't want to party all on my own. You're my mate. Take it."

"I don't suppose one little hit's gonna hurt me, is it?"

The feeling of defeat was drowned by oblivion. Jimmy lay back on his bunk, content with life for the first time in weeks. After lights out, Jimmy could hear Don coughing beneath him. He was on a binge.

"Better slow down, hadn't you?" Jimmy said. "You're in a mood tonight."

"I'm only just starting," Don replied. "I know what I'm

doing, don't I? Do you want another hit while there's still a bit left?"

"No. I'm sound." It had been so long since he'd done any that he didn't need any more. He fell asleep to a lullaby of sniffs and striking matches.

The noise of banging metal and locks and 'rise and shine' from the screws woke Jimmy as usual. Breakfast and work beckoned, so he jumped down to wake Don up.

"Time to get up mate," he said. "Another exciting day lies ahead."

There was no answer. Jimmy pulled the covers off him and grabbed his shoulder. Even through pyjamas, the skin was icy cold. Don was dead. The body turned, head lolling, eyes open and accusing. For a moment, Jimmy couldn't think who he was. The face seemed to form and reform as shadows of the past distorted the cold features. Frankie, Joey Godden, Frank Rogers, Tony Dixon . . . each took their turn. Then it was as if he was looking in a mirror. He saw the possibility of his own suicide staring him in the eye.

Chapter 27

The prison investigation was swift and thorough. The cause of death was obvious. Foil, matches and paper were lying under Don's hand. His body was carried out like it was riddled with the plague. As soon as the doctor had gone, two screws tore the cell apart while a third kept an eye on Jimmy. They didn't speak as they systematically took every picture off the wall, unstitched the pillows and dismantled the bed frames.

Then came the questioning and the recriminations. Jimmy was hauled before the governor and generally made to feel that he was to blame. This kind of thing wasn't good for the prison's reputation. The word on the grapevine was that the incident had been reported on national radio.

Jimmy took it all without comment. The row simply floated over him. He was too shocked to argue. Don had been his mate. The smack that killed him nearly went into Jimmy's system. In another mood, it could have been the other way round, with Jimmy bingeing and Don getting him to hold back.

He'd been brought right up against it. He'd smelt death, touched it with his hand. It cracked him up, even more than his own overdose. There was no one who could help. The screws dismissed him as just another junkie. The other inmates had their own problems.

Jackie was the only one he could talk to. He sent her a visiting order for the first time since he'd been there, preparing himself for disappointment. She came, reluctantly and suspiciously. Jimmy tried to take her hand, but she snatched it away.

"So," she said, angrily.

"So what?"

"So what the bloody hell do you want, Jimmy? Not a word from you since you've been in here. So why d'you suddenly want to see me? What're you after?"

Her attack took his breath away. His rehearsed explanations died on his lips. He came out with some banal statement about wanting to see how she was doing.

"Oh come on, Jimmy. What is it? Are you in some kind of trouble?"

"It's not like that. I just wanted to talk to you, love. I missed you."

"Three months. And you're only missing me now."

"No. I think about you every single day, Jack. It's doing me head in."

"So why didn't you send me a visiting order?"

"Because I didn't want you near this place. You've seen what it's like here. Look at it. The place is full of crooks."

"What did you expect?" At least she was smiling, in a grim sort of way. "Why the change of mind?"

"Something's happened. You probably heard about it on the news. This fella, Don Macagre, died of a drugs overdose in here."

The smile vanished as Jackie's voice went back to iron. "Oh yeah, I heard about it alright. Do you know what I thought? I thought it might have been you. Then when I heard this fella's name, I'm not sure if I was relieved or not, because I thought if it was you, then it might be the best thing for both of us. At least it would be over."

What could he say? It nearly was him. Slowly, hesitantly, he told her what had happened. He watched as her face went through disgust, anger, disbelief and, finally, sympathy. As he described how he'd touched the body, she took his hand, warming him for the first time in weeks.

"It could have been me, Jack," he ended. "That's why I needed to see you. It's cracking me up, seeing him like that. I'm never going to look at another drug again. I'm clean and I'm going to stay clean."

How many times had he made those kinds of promises? Yet Jackie seemed to know that this was it. He'd been shocked to the core, jolted out of himself, by what had happened. And she was with him. Ironically, it had taken Don's death to win her back.

Jimmy fetched them a nice, normal cup of tea and asked her how she was doing. The answer came back – barely coping.

"You left me without a stick of furniture in that house. I've had to buy things. Then there's all the bills you didn't pay."

What could he do but apologise and hang his head in shame?

"And I'm getting behind with the rent," she continued. "I was thinking of going to see Barry."

"No."

"I've got to get the money somehow."

"I don't want you scrounging it off Barry. I'll get you the money." His wife wasn't going to beg.

"How?"

"I've managed to save a few quid in here. They pay me for working in the kitchens. I'll get it, I promise you."

"I've heard your promises before."

"Jackie. Give me a bit of time, will you? I'll get the money for you."

"Alright, but it had better be quick."

Jimmy knew exactly where he could lay his hands on some dosh. Don's stash remained undiscovered. Obviously, he didn't intend to take it himself, but there were plenty of other mugs in there who'd sell their grandmothers for the stuff. Oscar and Brian's arguments came flooding back to him. If people wanted to ruin their lives and pay for it, who was he to stop them?

Walton Prison had a solid education programme, GCSE's in French, woodwork and beginner's drug dealing. There were all sorts of tricks and tips. Ways to distract the screws when there was a risk of them finding the stuff in your socks and how to tell when a raid was in the air. Jimmy put on his harmless act whenever he wanted to sell. Kick a football around a couple of times in the exercise yard and everyone thought you were a right goody goody.

In no time, Jimmy had set up shop, created his own little franchise. His place of business was the kitchen and his terms were twenty quid a time. Interest was charged at 10% per month and punters could either get their loved ones to bring money in or arrange for Jimmy to be paid when he got out. The stuff was good and the price wasn't too outrageous. Soon Jimmy had several regulars.

His old optimism was coming back. Full of self importance, Jimmy spotted a couple of likely customers hanging around the kitchen.

"What's it to be, lads?" he asked.

They grinned, then one drew back his fist and punched him

in the face. He didn't stand a chance. All he could do was curl up in a ball while they kicked the shit out of him. The crowning humiliation was when they tipped a pan of cold baked beans over his head.

It was soon over and he'd endured far worse. The message came through. That was a warning. He'd stepped on a couple of rather large toes. Don't do it again. Jimmy shrugged it off. So it was a bit of a painful lesson. He knew the limits now. As long as he stuck to his band of small fry and kept his head down, there was room for his operation.

Jimmy had a green notebook for recording all his transactions. As the pages filled up with money owed and money collected, he started to make plans for when he got out. When Don's stash ran out, it was easy to find another source.

To the authorities, James Corkhill was an excellent example of how the penal system ought to work. A wreck when he came in, the man was now fit and healthy, weaned off drugs, full of confidence and willing to co-operate. As soon as he was up for parole, an early release date was granted.

Jimmy decided not to tell Jackie and forbade Sinbad to, as well. The few pathetic quid he'd scraped together from the kitchen would stretch to a big bunch of flowers. When she came to visit, he only just managed to stop himself from spilling the beans.

"You seem in a good mood," she commented. "How come?"

"Why shouldn't I be?" he teased.

"You're in jail for a start." She peered closely at him. "You're high on something, aren't you?"

"I'm high on life. D'you wanna know why? Because I am getting out of here. They're letting me out early."

She wanted to know when, but he wasn't going to spoil the surprise.

"Soon," he said. "A couple of weeks. I can't wait to be back home with you, love. It's going to be great."

He had everything to look forward to. A wife who loved him and who'd stood by him. Not only was he off the smack, he was fit and healthy. Best of all, he had a new career making real money. Jackie would get her dream house. The one he'd always promised her.

A week later, he walked through the prison gates a happy man. His plans were settled. He was going to collect the money he was owed, check in with his new supplier and start looking for customers.

The days when he had to pester Brian Kennedy for contacts were over. He couldn't believe how naive he'd been then. Brian had always told him it was a doddle and it was. Especially when you'd just been in prison. The network of potential customers was wide and Jimmy had access to every corner of it.

He tapped his pocket, checking his notebook was still there. Putting his best foot forward, he headed for home.

HOW TO ORDER YOUR BOXTREE BOOKS

BROOKSIDE
1-85283-946-5	*Phil Redmond's Brookside: Life in the Close*	£14.99 hb
1-7522-0972-8	*Brookside: The Journals of Beth Jordache*	£4.99 pb

CORONATION STREET
1-85283-456-0	*Life and Times of Rovers Return*	£14.99 hb
1-85283-907-4	*Life and Times of Rovers Return*	£9.99 pb
0-7522-0870-5	*The Coronation Street Quiz Book*	£2.99 pb

THE BILL
1-85283-911-2	*The Bill: The First Ten Years*	£14.99 hb

EMMERDALE
1-85283-446-3	*Emmerdale 21 Years*	£9.99 pb
1-85283-922-8	*Emmerdale Family Album*	£13.99 hb

LONDON'S BURNING
1-85283-874-4	*London's Burning*	£9.99 pb
1-85283-731-4	*London's Burning*	£14.99 hb

SOLDIER, SOLDIER
1-85283-879-5	*Soldier, Soldier*	£14.99 hb
1-85283-480-3	*Soldier, Soldier*	£9.99 pb

Boxtree Cash Sales, P.O. Box 11, Falmouth, Cornwall TR10 9EN

Please send a cheque or postal order for the value of the book and add the following for postage and packing:

U.K. including B.F.P.O. – £1.00 for one book plus 50p for the second book, and 30p for each additional book ordered up to a £3.00 maximum.

Overseas including Eire – £2.00 for the first book plus £1.00 for the second book, and 50p for each additional book ordered.

OR please debit this amount from my Access/Visa Card (delete as appropriate).

Card Number

Amount £ ....

Expiry Date ....

Signed ....

Name ....

Address ....